SLAVES FOREVER?

The sentry herded Moshe and Kevin single file along the pathway toward a richly decorated tent.

Suddenly a giant man dressed in flowing Egyptian robes and gold armbands blocked their path and stood before them with his arms crossed. "Who are these people?" he demanded.

"I found them above the camp, Lord Korah. They may be spies," replied the sentry, trembling before the towering figure.

"Spies?" the man called Korah replied. He turned to Moshe and Kevin. "Do you know what we do to spies and pig worshipers?" he asked, snickering cruelly. With a flourish he drew a jeweled dagger from his belt and lunged at them....

Look for these other titles in the Pennypincher Series:

- Sports
  *Brad Benson and the Secret Weapon* by Steve Swanson
  *Batting Ninth for the Braves* by Nate Aaseng
  *42 Red on Four* by Nate Aaseng
- Animals
  *A Horse Named Cinnamon* by Jeanne Hovde
  *All Alone (Except for My Dog Friday)* by Claire Blatchford
- Bundy Street Gang Adventures
  *The Crooked Gate* by Marilyn Donahue
  *To Catch a Golden Ring* by Marilyn Donahue
  *The Music Plays Past Midnight* by Marilyn Donahue
- Other Times & Other Places
  *Code Red on Starship Englisia* by Mark A. Durstewitz
  *The Claw and the Spiderweb* by Valerie Reddix
- Interesting People
  *If You Love Me, Call Me Dorrie* by Bonnie Sours Smith

*A Time Twist Adventure:*
# Secret of the Silver Candlestick

## Margaret Wallworth

**Chariot Books**

Chariot Books is an imprint of David C. Cook Publishing Co.

David C. Cook Publishing Co., Elgin, Illinois 60120
David C. Cook Publishing Co., Weston, Ontario

MOSHE DRUMMOND AND THE SILVER CANDLESTICK
© 1984 by Margaret Wallworth

Cover photo by Jim Steere

First Printing, 1984
Printed in the United States of America
89 88 87 86 85 84   5 4 3 2 1

Library of Congress Cataloging in Publication Data

Wallworth, Margaret.
  The secret of the silver candlestick.
  (Pennypincher series)
  Summary: When two twelve-year-old boys find an ancient
menorah from Biblical times, they are swept back in time to Moses'
day and witness the rebellion of Korah.
    1. Korah (Biblical figure)—Juvenile fiction.
[1. Korah (Biblical figure)—Fiction. 2. Space and time—Fiction] I. Title.
PZ7.W1598Se  1984     [Fic]     83-26223
ISBN 0-89191-832-9

# Contents

# 1
# The Silver
# Candlestick

"Come on, Kevin," Moshe shouted up at the open window. "Mom and Dad are both lecturing this morning so the coast is clear. I'll show you what they brought back from the dig at Kadesh-Barnea. Real neat stuff!"

Kevin was on the street in seconds. "Do they *still* think they've found the place where God sent fire to destroy the guys that rebelled against Moses?"

The sarcasm in the other boy's voice did not escape Moshe. Both boys were the sons of archaeologists and both knew the Bible practically by heart. But Kevin—unlike Moshe—had no belief in the accounts of the supernatural. Moshe chose to reply to Kevin's question as if he hadn't heard the sarcasm.

"It's still just a theory," Moshe said, jogging beside his friend as they picked their way between the busy morning foot traffic along the Jaffa Road. "It will take more than one season to find any firm evidence of that particular miracle. So far there's plenty of stuff to show that there was a big encampment there about the time Moses and his people were trying to get into the land of Canaan."

Moshe had been born in Israel, and although his parents were Americans and his older brother Bill attended the American school, Moshe had been given a Hebrew name and went to Hebrew schools from the time he was three years old. The result was that he spoke Hebrew and Arabic as well as he spoke English and the only country he had ever known was Israel.

The Drummonds lived in an apartment above an empty storefront which they used as a warehouse and workroom. Moshe let them in with his key and led Kevin to a dark back room crammed with boxes along the back wall. Large rough tables in the center of the room were covered with dirt-encrusted artifacts in the first stages of cleaning and sorting. To the untrained eye, it was a roomful of junk. To the eyes of Kevin and Moshe, whose earliest playgrounds had been dusty excavation sites of the Holy Land, the cluttered tables held all the excitement of Aladdin's cave.

"Whew!" Kevin breathed, "look at that! Whole pots, it looks like, and ... wow!" Kevin caught his breath and stood staring openmouthed at a huge, black encrusted object at the front edge of one of the tables. The accumulation of 4,000 years of grime softened the outlines, but it was clearly a candleholder with seven stems.

"A menorah?" Kevin asked.

Moshe grunted assent. "A really early form, looks like," he said. "Three metal semicircles making the six side holders and the main stem making the seventh. The base looks pointed, sort of, like it was meant to be stuck in the ground."

"Silver, from the looks of it," said Kevin, gingerly fingering the blackened crust. A mischievous grin flashed across his face. "Unless it's black from the fire of heaven," he cracked.

The humor missed Moshe who was gazing at the ancient object.

"No," he said, "you can tell by looking that the black is silver oxide, not carbon."

Kevin laughed. "You were serious!" he roared. "You really think fire from heaven is a possibility. Your folks are scientists. It beats me how any of you can believe in anything as unprovable as heaven and God and all that stuff."

"And it beats me," Moshe retorted, "how you and your folks can keep an open mind to all the possibilities of archaeology and shut out the most exciting idea of all—God and his hand in history."

"Spare me the testimonial," Kevin sighed, "and let's get back to the interesting stuff." He put his hand on the menorah again. "I'll bet this thing really looked impressive when it was standing up. Here, let's see if we can get it to stand." Kevin picked up the ancient candlestick and carried it with effort towards some sawhorses stacked in a corner of the storeroom.

"Hey, be careful. That thing is about 4,000 years old," Moshe protested. "I just wanted you to look, not handle the stuff!"

Kevin had hooked one of the sawhorses out of the stack with his foot. "Look, you get another one and we'll prop it in between here. I'll never take my hands off it. Besides, there's a nice soft pile of tarps here in case I do drop it. I'll bet that it was impressive when it was all silver and glinting in the sun."

"Or in the light and shadow of candlelight," Moshe offered, caught up in his friend's mood.

9

"Wait, I'll get underneath and hold it so you can step back and look at it."

Moshe crawled beneath the sawhorses and held the menorah from below. Kevin released his hold and stepped back a little.

"Doesn't seem right they'd stick something like that in the ground," he mused.

"Help!" Moshe shouted. "It's starting to slip and I can't hold it! Quick, Kevin ..."

Kevin hurled himself forward to grab the toppling candlestick, but whether he slipped on some slick spot or simply lost his balance, instead of catching the menorah, he slid feet first underneath the arch of the sawhorses, ramming into Moshe who grunted hard and lost his precarious hold on the precious artifact.

"Oh, no!" Moshe wailed, but instantly the menorah was out of their minds as they felt their bodies being sucked through some sort of windy passage, like money cartridges in a pneumatic tube at the bank. The storeroom dissolved in a blur of light, like the image on an overexposed negative. A terrific roaring drowned out their voices and, when at last the roaring stopped, their ears continued to hear the echo of it. They may have passed out because the next thing they knew, they were lying in darkness and everything was still.

"Kevin?"

"I'm right here, Moshe." Kevin's voice was very near and very frightened. "What happened to the lights?"

"I don't know," Moshe said. "What happened to the menorah, the sawhorses and my mom and dad's storeroom? Here's a tarp, but this isn't concrete underneath it. This is desert."

Kevin spread his arms. One touched Moshe and the other touched what felt like a rock face.

"I think we're in a cave," he said. "Let's join hands so we don't lose each other and see if we can find a way out."

The boys joined hands and felt gingerly along the rock. Suddenly the rock was gone and there was only empty air under their groping fingers. A breeze ruffled their hair. Both boys were sweating and the sudden gust of wind felt good to them.

"What's a breeze doing in a cave?" asked Kevin.

"Not to mention the stars," said Moshe. "Look up."

Kevin raised his eyes to the spangled sky. "How did we do that?" he exclaimed.

"We never were in a cave," said Moshe. "Look behind us. More sky on tha side. We were standing under a rock, or more accurately, under a rock formation shaped like an archway. Our eyes just hadn't had time to get used to the starlight. We're in the desert all right. Hear the jackals?"

They stood still. The whine of jackals sounded faintly.

"Let's just lie down here like Jacob from Bible times and pull up a couple of rocks for pillows. Then we'll see if we can figure out our directions from the stars."

"Neat idea," agreed Kevin, who knew the constellations of the Palestine sky as well as Moshe knew Hebrew. "We'll just find the Dipper and the North Star and take it from there."

The boys lay for a while in silence, searching for the familiar outlines. It was a frequent pleasure of theirs to lie on a Jerusalem rooftop and see who could find the constellations the quickest. Now, however, their silence continued for an abnormally long time. It was Kevin who finally spoke.

"They're all wrong," he said. Moshe could hear the clutch of panic in his friend's voice. "The constellations are all wrong."

Moshe felt a cold wave of horror spread through his limbs. He was glad that he was already lying down, for he didn't think his legs would have held him.

"There are constellations there that were never there before," Kevin whispered. "Look at that! The Hydra looks more like an octopus with all those extra strings of stars—and there are really bright stars between the Big Dipper and the Twins ..."

Kevin's voice faltered and died. Moshe felt a shiver of alarm. "Kevin, what's the matter? What is it?"

Kevin's voice shook. "What month is it, Moshe?"

"What month is it? September, of course. Why?"

"It *was* September," Kevin said vaguely. "Last night and the night before when I watched the stars, all the autumn constellations were in place."

"Well?" Moshe was impatient. He enjoyed stargazing in an uncomplicated way and could pick out the North Star as well as Kevin, but the details of shifting constellations didn't much interest him. "What does September have to do with anything?"

"There aren't just a few extra stars up there," Kevin explained. "Those are the spring constellations. Last night it was autumn and tonight it's spring. What's going on anyway?"

Again Moshe was glad to be lying down. An incredible thought was beginning to grow in his mind. "Kevin?" he asked tentatively. "Is it possible that, say a long time ago, there were stars up there that aren't there anymore?"

"Sure," said Kevin, "stars go out all the time. First they go prenova, then supernova, then *blooey*, they're dead. No more light. Some astronomers think that the star of Bethlehem was a supernova. Of course it could have been dead thousands, maybe millions, of years before anyone on earth saw it."

Warming to a favorite subject, Kevin had forgotten his panic of moments before. "Starlight takes so many years to reach the earth that every star up there could be dead and we wouldn't know it yet. The farther away the star or planet is, the longer its light takes to get here. If Jupiter were to blow up this minute, it would be thirty-five minutes before we'd know it. If the dog star went out, it'd be four years or so before anybody down here would notice."

"Is it possible that a long time ago, say in the time of Moses, there were stars up there that aren't there now—I mean in our own time?"

Kevin did not speak for several minutes. Moshe could sense the struggle as the same incredible idea took hold in his friend's mind.

"You mean you think that we've gone back in time?" Kevin almost shrieked and leapt to his feet.

Moshe stood up, too. "You know all the funny stuff started happening when the menorah from the Exodus site fell on us. My guess is that we're in a different time, maybe as far back as Moses."

Both boys scanned the dim landscape around them, looking for some clue to the period of time they were in. Only the barren desert shapes that had remained the same for thousands of years met their straining eyes.

Kevin saw the light first. "Look, over there," he said, pointing. "Do you see a light along the horizon?"

Moshe looked. "Yes, a kind of flickering, over that way."

Kevin gave a little jump and hooted.

"A highway! I'll bet you it's the highway from Jerusalem to Joppa!"

The boys started off at a quick trot towards the light. Moshe dragged the tarp along with him. How they got from the Drummond storeroom into the desert, was a question they did not allow to interfere with their moment of hope.

# 2

# "Where Are We?"

Even with their dark-adapted eyes, the boys found the going uncertain and several times one or the other turned an ankle on a bank of loose stones.

"It doesn't look like car lights," Kevin said as they neared the glow that had given them such hope.

Moshe grunted in agreement. "Looks more like firelight," he said. "Campfires." With a sudden cry Moshe lost his footing and slid among a clatter of stones that sounded fearfully loud in the silence. Kevin grabbed for him and arrested his fall down an embankment.

"Lucky for you it wasn't really steep," Kevin whispered, panting heavily.

Hearts pounding, the boys gazed at the scene that spread out below. Dark masses that could only be tents, loomed in the darkness. Here and there campfires flickered eerily. The boys could discern no human movement, but the presence of thousands of living peple made their skin prickle as with an electrical charge. They listened. The fear of the unknown quickened their senses. The barnyard smell of animals came to them on the night breeze and they heard the muffled bleat of goats or sheep shifting in their sleep.

"They're sure to have sentries or night watchmen, or whatever," said Kevin, "but we must not have made as much noise as we thought."

The boys strained to see the outlines of the camp.

"Looks pretty big," Moshe said, "and back there, that big dark mass seems to be trees. I can't think of any wadi that big, except maybe one of the new oases in the Negev. And there wouldn't be that many Bedouins in the area to account for all those tents."

Kevin exhaled a sigh that was almost a sob. "I don't even want to think about it anymore," he said, drawing back from the edge of the embankment. "Let's find someplace where we can stay till it's light."

They cast about for some kind of shelter. A low, dark shape about ten yards away proved to be a clump of weathered stone similar to the formation under which they had been thrust into the desert landscape.

"I'm glad you brought along the tarp," Kevin said as they burrowed into one of the larger crevices. "I'm beginning to feel cold."

For a long time the boys stared at the lights beyond and below them.

"Who do you suppose they are?" Kevin asked.

Moshe shook his head. "Until we know for sure where we are and when we are, it's not much use trying to guess who they are."

"You're right," Kevin said gloomily. "Guess the only thing to do is try to get some sleep and hope for the best." Soon Kevin's even breathing told Moshe he was asleep. At least Kevin's fears were at rest for a little while.

Moshe lay awake thinking about their situation. Unlike Kevin, he could do more than hope for the best. He could pray. Summoning all his faith in a watchful creator present in the world since the beginning of time, Moshe prayed for protection and help. There, in the cold desert darkness, Moshe felt a warm sense of security settle over him like a blanket. He shut his eyes against the campfires of the unknown people on the wadi below and slept.

The clatter of dislodged stones woke Moshe and Kevin at the same instant. Some instinct kept them from moving or crying out. Not three feet from where they huddled in the crevice stood a man in the dress of a desert nomad, his back to them. He was standing where the boys had stood earlier, looking over the encampment. Slowly he turned his gaze, sweeping their stone hiding place without seeing them. He was a short man, swathed in several layers of tunics and robes. On his head he wore a rough woven headdress of different dull colors fastened by a black cord that glistened like animal hair as he moved. His face, in the shadows of the headdress, was swarthy and cruel. A scar ran from his left nostril, under his left eye, and disappeared into the folds of the head covering. He carried a spear. Seeing nothing, he spat and walked away. Hardly breathing, the boys listened to his receding footsteps.

"Whew!" Kevin breathed when the footsteps had been gone for several minutes. "Not exactly what you'd call a friendly looking face."

"He looked like a Bedouin, but then again, he didn't."

Kevin nodded. "I don't know what the difference was," he said, "but I had the same feeling."

It was the clothes," Moshe said. "Not any of his

stuff was store-bought; all of it looked rough woven or made out of animal hair or rough dressed skins. No fancy leather straps with brass buckles. And that spear. When's the last time you saw a Bedouin armed with anything but a rifle?"

Kevin huddled miserably in the tarp.

"I'd say let's get out of here, but where can we go? If everyone is as mean as that guy looked, they'd as soon stick us like a couple of pigs as give us directions."

"If wishes were worth anything," grunted Moshe, disentangling himself from the tarp and stretching his aching limbs, "I'd wish we had put a few miles between us and this place while it was still dark. As it is, I vote for getting away right now. If we ..."

Moshe never finished his thought. The sudden force of a blow against his ribs sent him hurtling to the ground, the breath knocked out of him. The cruel-looking nomad was standing over him brandishing the blunt end of his spear and speaking angrily in some unintelligible language. It was not Hebrew or Arabic or any other language Moshe could recognize. The nomad's motions, however, spoke as clearly as any words and Moshe stumbled to his feet as Kevin came out of the crevice. The tarp from the storeroom was still tangled around the other boy like a garment and when he tried to disengage himself from it, their captor made threatening gestures with the pointed end of his spear.

"He may think you're trying to get a weapon," Moshe suggested, "better wear it. It probably looks more like normal clothing to him than what I'm wearing."

Both boys were dressed in khaki shorts and cotton shirts. Moshe's shirt was plain tan to match his shorts. Under his tarp Kevin was wearing an American style

T-shirt sent to him by a cousin who was at a university in the state of Arkansas. Moshe recalled that the shirt was a bright red with some sort of design in white. Kevin had on sandals without socks; Moshe was wearing tennis shoes and plain white crew socks.

The sentry, if that is what he was, herded the boys before him, still shouting words in the unrecognizable language.

"He seems to be saying the same words over and over. Ow!" Moshe stumbled under another painful prod of the spear. "How come he just pokes me with that thing? Have you noticed that he never touches you?"

"Coincidence," muttered Kevin, "or short arms. You're closer to him than I am."

"No. I think it's the tarp."

Kevin scowled at his friend.

"Very funny," he said. "Here we are being marched probably to our deaths and you're making jokes about the way I'm dressed."

"No," Moshe insisted. "I'm serious. Look at how they're dressed."

By now they had descended the slope and had reached the fringes of the camp where nomads of every age stopped what they were doing to stare at the strange prisoners.

"See?" Moshe said, waving an arm at the curious bystanders, who ducked and made some kind of countersign as if trying to avoid a curse. "Only the children are barelegged," Moshe pointed out. "Children and the poverty-stricken men. Our guard must think you're the master because with that tarp, you're dressed more like the important-looking ones. In these shorts at my age I must look like a slave. That's why I'm getting the butt end of that spear and you're not."

The bystanders fell away on either side as the

sentry herded his captives single file along the pathway between the tents. Abruptly Kevin stopped. Ahead of them, blocking the path, was a man dressed for all the world like a worshiper in an Egyptian tomb painting. His Egyptian headdress had a winged circle on it. His arms were banded with gold bracelets and at his neck he wore a wide torque of gold, set with blue stones. He stood at least a head taller than the sentry. His nose was large and hooked, his forehead high. His whole bearing displayed an authority that would not be questioned. He spoke haughtily to the sentry and Moshe realized with a thrill that he could understand the man's words.

"What are these and where are you taking them?" he demanded.

The man with the spear responded in the same tongue. His voice was no longer angry, but subdued, almost placating.

"I found them above the camp, Lord Korah, and I am taking them to Caleb's tent. They may be spies from the land beyond. I spoke to them in the language of the Egyptians, but they show no understanding of it."

"I will take them now," the man called Korah replied. "You may go back to your place."

"But my lord Korah," the man protested. "Caleb bid us all to bring all strangers directly to him or to Joshua."

Korah's eyes blazed under his rich headdress. He pushed past the two boys and stood above the sentry who cowered before him. "Get out of here, dog! Caleb does not rule among the tents of Korah. Go!"

Fear in every line of his body, the sentry turned back the way he had come, deprived of his prizes. The boys stood uncertainly as their new captor

19

looked them over. His eyes settled on Kevin who still wore the tarpaulin.

"Do you understand the speech of the people?" he asked.

Kevin stared blankly and Moshe moved closer to him, speaking quickly in English.

"He's speaking some funny kind of Hebrew," Moshe said. "He thinks you're the master. Better say something first and then I'll do the talking."

Kevin looked pale. "What should I say?"

"Say you're from a far country and your servant will speak for you."

"What servant?"

"Me, of course. Go ahead. He looks like he's getting annoyed."

Kevin looked up at Korah. Frantically he reached into his meager store of Hebrew. He had reluctantly studied four years of Hebrew in school . It was just another subject to be learned for a test and never used.

"I am from a country away from here, far," he said haltingly. "My worker here (he couldn't think of the word for *servant*) to speak for me."

"You will come with me to my tent," Korah said. "I would hear more of your country and why you are here."

Swishing and jingling magnificently, Korah swept before them and the boys followed quickly after.

"Maybe he'll give us something to eat," Kevin whispered to Moshe.

Moshe nodded, but as hungry as he was, his thoughts were not on food. The names that had passed between the sentry and Korah kept ringing in his mind. Caleb and Joshua. Impossible as it was, he and Kevin had traveled backwards in time. There was no doubt now in his mind. They were in the camp of Moses!

# 3
# Pig Worshipers

The interior of Korah's tent was dim and smelled of spices, incense, and perfume. The winged disk of Korah's headdress was repeated on a tent hanging and on a three-legged, bronze stand that held glowing coals. Thin wisps of smoke rose from the coals. Moshe wondered why the winged disk seemed so familiar. He knew he had seen the symbol before, but he couldn't remember where or in what connection.

Two young boys stood alertly at the entrance of the tent, glancing only furtively at Moshe and Kevin, their main attention on Korah as if afraid to miss his slightest word or gesture.

"Sit," Korah commanded, motioning to some cushions in the center of the tent. Kevin sat down awkwardly, because he was still swathed with the tarp. Moshe squatted beside him, not wishing to provoke Korah before he had a chance to explain that he was not in fact a slave.

Korah clapped his hands and the two servant

boys moved instantly to bring a basin of water and towels. They removed Kevin's sandals with difficulty because of the buckles, but made no move to touch Moshe's tennis shoes. Much to Kevin's astonished embarrassment, the young servants washed his feet in the sweetly scented water, dried them carefully, and rubbed them with some kind of spicy-smelling salve.

"What are they doing?" Kevin asked in a sharp whisper. Moshe made an effort not to laugh.

"They're washing your feet," he replied, "like in the Bible. Their master considers you an equal. He's being hospitable."

"Yuck," said Kevin.

With the foot washing complete, Korah gave a short, gruff order and the servants came back with a plate of what looked like flat biscuits and two flasks. The drink poured for Kevin was the same as that poured for Korah—dark and sweet-smelling wine, Moshe guessed. Moshe, however, was given a bowl of water.

"Now," said Korah as Kevin put the drink to his lips, "I will hear of your country and lineage."

Kevin recoiled from the taste in the cup, but Moshe leaned close and whispered, "Pretend to like it."

Korah watched them expectantly. Cautiously Moshe made a little bow and spoke.

"My lord Korah is very gracious to these poor travelers from a far country. It is my friend's wish ..."

Korah started at the word "friend," but Moshe went on, determined to clear up the misunderstanding that Kevin was his master.

"My friend's wish is to inform you that we are both sons of free men. Our fathers are ..." he searched for the equivalent of the word "colleague." "Our fathers work together in our own country. We left

22

unexpectedly. We had no time to take thought for our clothing."

Korah nodded. His eyes seemed to glint with understanding. "Stolen?" he asked. "Our ancestor Joseph was stolen in such a way from his father's house. By his own brothers was he stripped of his beautiful coat and sold naked to the Egyptians."

Korah paused to clap and the servants again brought water, this time to wash Moshe's feet. Sinking onto a cushion beside Kevin, Moshe felt a little of Kevin's embarrassment, but the touch of the water on his hot feet was so pleasant and refreshing that he quickly gave himself up to the enjoyment of it. *How very special it makes one feel,* he thought, *to have someone washing your feet.* No wonder the disciples were so touched when Jesus knelt to wash theirs.

"You are not Egyptians?" Korah asked.

"No," Moshe said, "we are Americans."

Korah frowned and stiffened. "Kinsmen of the Amalekites?"

"Oh, no," Moshe said quickly, recalling the enmity between the Hebrews and the Amalekites during the settling of the Promised Land. "We are not from the lands near here. Our home lies many months away, across large waters."

Korah looked puzzled. "Many months? This is difficult to comprehend. How then, do you know the speech of our people? For though you speak it badly, nevertheless you speak it."

Moshe thought rapidly. It was plain that Korah was suspicious of their story. His hospitality could turn any moment to dangerous hostility.

"We lived some time in the land beyond," Moshe said, using the term he had heard the sentry use. "My teacher was of your people."

Korah nodded slowly. "It could be," he said.

"Perhaps not all the people went down into Egypt with our father Joseph. Some may have remained behind in the land of the pig worshipers."

Korah sat for a while in silence, evidently deciding what to do with the strangers. Finally he barked a command to the servant boys. They went to a corner of the tent and came back with articles of clothing.

"For now I will regard you as my guests," Korah said. "Here are garments more suited to freeborn men than what you now wear. At the next meeting I will take you before the elders. You will have much useful information about the land beyond." Korah laughed mirthlessly. "Indeed, you will have a wealth of information that will put our brave spies Joshua and Caleb to shame."

Moshe and Kevin rose to allow the servants to dress them. Moshe quickly removed his tank top and walking shorts and stood waiting in his undershorts. The servants pointed at them in some surprise and said something to one another.

"What do you suppose they're going on about?" Kevin asked.

"Underwear hasn't been invented yet," Moshe said. He clung firmly to his shorts and at last the servants slipped a long, soft gown like the one Korah was wearing over his head. It was of a fine woven cloth, probably wool, Moshe guessed, and dyed a delicate pale blue.

While the servants attended Moshe and Kevin, another person entered the tent and sat down beside Korah. Moshe observed even in the shadowy light of the tent this man's face was without the lines of cruelty so evident in those of the sentry or Korah. Much younger than Korah, he possessed the same dignity and, though his attitude was respectful, it was not at all servile.

The servants now removed the tarp that Kevin had been wearing over his shorts and T-shirt since their capture. As the tarp slid to the ground, the servants gasped. Korah glanced up and his features contorted into a mask of outrage. The young man's face registered surprise and disgust and both he and Korah got to their feet. Korah drew a jeweled dagger from his belt and strode purposefully towards Kevin. Moshe stood frozen, certain that his friend was about to be killed outright and perhaps himself with him. Kevin stood helplessly watching Korah advance. His red T-shirt was dark in the uncertain light of the tent, but the white design on it gleamed. The design was that of a razorback hog, the snarling, charging boar that is the university mascot in Arkansas. With his left hand Korah grabbed the front of the T-shirt and slashed it in two. Then he took the shirt at the back, pulled it roughly off of Kevin's arms and flung it at one of the cowering servants.

"Burn it!" he shouted, "Burn the abomination and bring water. The tent and all in it are unclean. Unclean!" Turning back to Moshe and Kevin, he knocked them both to the ground.

"Slaves!" he shouted. "How dare you bring your foul pig into my tent?" He kicked furiously at Moshe. "Remove that garment from him and purify it," he ordered the servants. "Give them both the rags of slaves. They are your fellow bondsmen now, not your betters."

With a roughness in extreme contrast to the reverent gentleness with which they had dressed him, the servants pulled the finely woven gown from Moshe and threw a coarse strip of fabric at him. Glancing at the slaves to see how the thing was worn, Moshe wrapped it around his hips like a long bath towel and tucked the end in at his waist. Kevin was made to remove his walking shorts and he, too, wrapped one of the long garments around himself. Barefoot and barebacked, both boys were driven from the tent. Korah's voice could be heard roaring after them.

"Take them to Eber. Tell him to find work for them. His is a craft fit for swine worshipers!"

So abrupt and complete was the change in the manner of the two servant boys, Moshe stared at them, imagining that the two who had so gently washed their feet in Korah's tent had been replaced by two others whose every touch was a blow and whose mouths never stopped uttering curses.

"Move, you sons of swines," snarled one. "Thanks to you we're unclean until sundown."

"Aye," shouted the other, "and we must wash everything in Lord Korah's tent."

One of the servants led, followed by Kevin and Moshe, while the other servant brought up the rear. He had no spear with which to prod, but both Moshe and Kevin felt his fist or his foot.

This time no one lined the pathway to stare. Instead there was a constant flurry of motion as women and children scattered at their approach. Soon they were out of the camp going east. Passing the last of the tents, Kevin and Moshe and their keepers headed downhill over a bare stretch of rocky ground towards an isolated clump of trees.

"Ow!" exclaimed Kevin. "They could have given us back our shoes at least."

A sudden barking heralded the approach of an ill-looking pack of dogs. The servant boys stooped quickly, caught up rocks and hurled them at the advancing dogs, which at once turned tail and ran off yelping.

"What's that awful smell?" Kevin said as they neared the clump of trees.

Moshe took a breath and wrinkled his nose in disgust.

"Smells like something dead."

A few more steps brought them in view of a small cluster of tents. Black acrid smoke rose from a fire at some distance from the largest tent, and a few yards away from the fire a man dressed like themselves leaned over what looked like a waterskiing platform, pushing something back and forth with the motions of a woman using a washboard.

"Eber!" shouted one of the servants, stopping at a distance. "We bring you two helpers from the lord Korah. He bids you use them as you will. They are foul pig worshipers never to be redeemed."

The man's brown face split into a grin.

"Good, good. I need some extra hands around here. Lamech has a strong back, but there is more work than we can handle between us. Not too many youngsters are eager to help the tanner."

As Eber came forward, the two servants backed away. The tanner laughed.

"If they be pig worshipers indeed, then you're already unclean, my boys. No need to back off from old Eber."

With a swift movement, the man leapt forward and swatted each servant on the head. With looks of horror and disgust on their faces, they scurried away like the dogs they had routed a moment before. The tanner laughed uproariously.

"Mustn't touch a tanner. Oh, no, a tanner's unclean from all the dead animals he handles. Well, unclean or not, what would they do without their straps and waterskins and sandals? Come along, lads, you look likely enough. Ever lent a hand at tanning?"

Moshe, with effort, could understand the rough Hebrew of the tanner. "No, sir," he said, "we've never even seen the work done."

"Never seen the work done. Oh, no, well, you wouldn't, your being such fine gentlemen and all might get a mite faint from the smell." Again the man laughed, delighted with his own sense of humor. "Come along, then," he said, turning back to where he had been working. "I'll give you your first lesson in the mystery of preparing hides."

Moshe and Kevin hung back. The smell that lay over Eber's ground was sickening. The grin left Eber's face.

"Come now, don't go all dainty on me. Wherever you're from, my fine young laddies, you know what has happened to you by now." He stood looking them over, impatient lines forming on his dark face.

"What's he saying?" Kevin asked. "I can only make out about every tenth word. What's he want us to do? I can't stand the stink, Moshe. Let's get out of here." Kevin made a move to go. Eber put out a thick sinewed hand and closed it over Kevin's wrist. Moshe saw his friend wince at the pressure of the grip.

"We can't go," Moshe said weakly. "I'm not sure exactly whom we belong to, but we're not free to do what we want to anymore."

Kevin blanched under his tan. "You mean we're … we're …" He could not finish and fell silent.

Moshe nodded miserably. "Slaves," he finished for him. "We're slaves."

"Come," ordered Eber, "I'll show you what you must do."

Slowly Kevin and Moshe followed Eber over to the evil-smelling skins on which he had been working.

"This will be your job," the tanner explained, handing them each a sharp implement like a bowed knife. "You will scrape off whatever is left of the fat on the underside of the skin. These have already had the hairs removed." Eber spat. "At least as much of the hair as can be removed in these miserable conditions. In Egypt, now, there a tanner could ply his craft. Proper tanning pits there and lime and bark and running water."

Moshe took the tool. Kevin, however, turned away and was sick.

"You'll get used to it," Eber said. "It's always harder when you're not born to it as I was."

Holding his breath as long as he could against the smell, Moshe began to scrape.

# 4
# A Knife in the Night

Moshe scraped until he thought his arms would drop off at the shoulders. Kevin overcame his nausea and Eber put him to work stirring hides in a big pit. Sweating and straining for what seemed an eternity, the boys labored under the tanner's eyes until the sun was at its zenith. Then Eber called them from their tasks and led them to a shady spot on the far side of his tent. Here the stench did not seem so oppressive and the boys reached eagerly for the bowls of water that Eber had poured for them.

"Hot work, tanning," said Eber, leaning back on a pile of finished skins and biting into a piece of dark bread. "You lads are still a mite tender, but you'll do, you'll do. That stirring will give you a strong back, eh, lad?" Eber laughed and punched Kevin, who did not smile. Moshe translated what the tanner had said.

"Hmph," grunted Kevin. "You don't need to translate for me. I got the gist of it. Strong back, Ha! Another day like that and I'll have no back at all."

"Where's your regular helper?" Moshe asked Eber.

"Out gathering dung," Eber replied.

"Dung?"

Eber nodded. "Jackal dung. Does better than dog dung although I use dog when I can't get better. In Egypt, now!" Eber swallowed a mouthful of water and sighed. "Lord Moses can say what he will about the Egyptians. I've seen my old master Hotep turn out leather soft as a baby's skin. You can bet he didn't do it with jackal dung. Jars and jars of special stuff he had, oil, alum, lime, grape juice. Once he sent me all over Tanis to find a yellow she-goat. He wanted the milk to tan a goat's skin. Had to be a yellow one, mind you." Chuckling at the recollection, Eber shook his head.

"Cunning, those Egyptians," he said. "Know more about dead things than an honest man knows about the living. Do you know that they can take the corpse of a man and tan the whole thing so it will last hundreds of years?"

"More like thousands, you mean," said Kevin with a mouthful of barley cake, pleased to have understood some of the conversation. Moshe shot him a warning glance, but the tanner had not heard.

"Fact is," said Eber, "we have such an Egyptian corpse right here in the camp." He looked at Moshe's startled expression with satisfaction.

"It's our ancestor Joseph himself," he said.

"Of course!" exclaimed Moshe, then bit off his words. It would never do to reveal how much knowledge of the Hebrews they had. It might condemn them as spies on the one hand or as fortune-tellers on the other. Either way they would be in danger of being executed.

"Where is this body?" Moshe asked carefully. "It is a sight I would dearly love to see."

"And so would a lot of other folks in the camp," said Eber. "Moses hid it. Nobody knows where he's put it. Put back with the rest of the extra baggage his sister Miriam brought away from Egypt most likely."

"But why?" Moshe asked, "with something as precious as the body of Joseph, I'd have thought you'd have it in some place of honor, like its own special tent or something."

"So we did," Eber said, "when we first came out. Carried it behind the Ark, we did, and put up a tent for it right beside the Tabernacle."

"Well?" demanded Moshe. "What happened?"

"Folks started worshiping it," said Eber. "Started putting little offerings of wine and bread and so on outside the tent. Old Korah even went and prayed by it with incense once—big on incense is Korah. He doesn't feel like a prayer's a prayer without it. Well, old Moses nearly broke his staff for sure that time. Called a big meeting, said a body's a body, not a god. And don't no Hebrew pray to anyone or anything only to the one true God, him whose name no man is allowed to speak. Next day there was no trace of the tent or the coffin. It's out of sight, Moses says, until we get into the Promised Land where we'll bury it proper, not to be dug up again like a dead Egyptian."

His tale at an end, Eber stretched luxuriously. "Time for afternoon rest," he said. "You can sleep anywhere you like. Wouldn't try to run off, though," he added, divining the thought that sprang into the boys' minds. "Lamech there would have you back in a jiffy. Lamech never sleeps."

Moshe and Kevin whirled round to see if Eber was tricking them or if, in fact, someone was behind them. It was no trick. A tall, thick-necked man stood not three feet away. His approach had been completely soundless.

"Lamech, meet our new slaves," said Eber pleasantly. "Lord Korah sent them to us. If they don't behave, they must answer to him."

"Scrawny as girls," grunted Lamech.

"They'll fatten up," Eber said easily. "Plenty of goats' milk and plenty of work, they'll be a help to us both. Any luck?"

Lamech shrugged. "Two basketfuls," he said. He snatched at the remains of the lunch, devouring the fragments like an animal.

"Take your rest, Lamech," said Eber. "Lord Moses has said that everyone in the camp, man and beast, bond and free, should take the afternoon rest lest they be worked past exhaustion."

Lamech spat. "Dathan is my lord, not Moses," he said sullenly. "Lord Dathan wants the skin by sundown. He says there will be no food unless he receives it by nightfall. It is ready for the last oiling. I will do it now." Lamech padded off to the work area, wiping his mouth with the back of his hand.

"Not much personality," observed Kevin in his broken Hebrew.

Ēber shook his head and closed his eyes. "Lamech is a strange one," he agreed, "but tanners can't be too particular. The work doesn't attract the flower of Israel, you might say. He does the work." Eber's words ended in a snore and he was asleep.

"Want to make a run for it?" Kevin whispered.

Moshe looked doubtfully at the open spaces beyond the tannery.

"We'd do better at night," he said. "Lamech looks as strong as a bull. He could break our necks with a swat of his hand."

Kevin nodded.

"From the stony look in his eye I'd bet he could do it with no more thought than if we were a couple of flies. I don't think I've ever seen a meaner-looking man. Even the sentry that brought us in looks like a teddy bear compared to Lamech."

"Better get some rest while we can," Moshe said.

Exhausted by the grueling labor of the morning, Moshe and Kevin closed their eyes and slept.

The sun was lower in the sky when Eber nudged the boys awake with his foot.

"Back to work, lads," he ordered cheerfully. "We have two new hides with Aaron's mark on them. I'll show you how to get them started. But first put these on." He threw them each a pair of sandals, which they put on gladly.

Eber worked closely with the boys all afternoon, instructing them in his craft while Lamech worked alone at a distance from them. The work was hard, tedious, and disagreeable, but Eber was a cheerful, talkative man and not unreasonable. He demanded nothing of the boys without first demonstrating how a thing should be done. Between instructions he delivered a constant stream of observations about events and personalities so that by suppertime the boys knew not only how to trim and clean a hide for curing, they knew quite a lot of gossip.

Lamech, for example, had a mysterious past. According to Eber he had come out of Egypt under the protection of Dathan.

"Some say he's not a Hebrew," Eber told them, "but an Egyptian who killed someone in his master's house and had to flee. No matter, here he's a free man. Dathan would have set him up with a flock, or so they say. But personally," said Eber, leaning forward and lowering his voice, "I think Lamech fears and hates Dathan. Someday I'll tell you why. But not now. Why he chose to be a tanner is beyond me. Tanning is the worst job in the tribe."

The boys looked at each other. Obviously Eber did

not want to talk about Lamech anymore.

"Why are you a tanner, Eber?" Moshe couldn't help asking.

"My father was," Eber replied simply. "It never occurred to me to be anything else."

Eber showed the boys where to wash. Then, lifting his hands to heaven, he stood with his back to the setting sun and prayed.

"Don't you have a wife, Eber?" Kevin asked, when they were all squatting round the meal.

"I had a wife," said Eber. "A son, too; a fine, likely lad. They both belong to another man now."

Eber ate for a long while in silence, apparently lost in painful recollection. "Sarah married me knowing my trade," he said finally. "But she couldn't know until she had lived with me whether or not she could bear it."

Eber sighed. "It was when our son was born," he went on sadly. "She said she could bear it for herself, but that when she thought of that little child growing up with the stench of dead animals all around him she just couldn't do it. The boy would be always unclean and never allowed to enter the congregation at worship, she said. She set her heart against me. So I released her, saying to the council that she displeased me."

Eber finished his meal in silence. Neither Moshe nor Kevin wished to intrude on his personal sorrow, so they, too, refrained from talking. Lamech came up and sat hunched over his meal of cheese, curds, and barley bread with a sullen scowl on his rough features.

"Pah!" he exclaimed, tearing at a piece of bread with his teeth. "Nothing here fit for a man to eat. Just manna every day. And Dathan cheats me out of my fair portion. A man needs meat."

Eber awoke from his reverie. "Even a man with

many flocks does not eat meat every day," he said. "The man who kills his flocks for meat destroys his substance."

"Pah!" Lamech spat again, vehemently, "a man doesn't have to kill a sheep to enjoy mutton," he said and left them.

Kevin stared after him. "What do you suppose he meant by that?" he asked Moshe.

"I haven't a clue," Moshe said. "Maybe it's some sort of ancient proverb."

Eber, however, also stared after Lamech, a disturbed frown wrinkling his forehead.

Supper over, exhaustion flooded over the unaccustomed slaves and Eber showed them where they would sleep—two mats on the earth floor of his tent. "Don't try to run off," he warned. "Lamech spreads his mat at the entrance."

Moshe sank down on the mat. "Don't worry," he said, "I may never move again!"

Eber laughed. "You'll move all right," he said. "A slave has no choice but to move when his master says move."

Moshe let his body relax, feeling the relief of one who has worked hard all day and knows that he has earned eight hours of undisturbed sleep. Sleep. Macbeth had it right, he thought vaguely as his mind closed down. Sleep, chief nourisher in life's feast ..."

It seemed only a moment later when Moshe felt someone shake him. "Up! Get up! Now!"

It was Eber's voice, insistent, harsher than they had heard it up until then.

"Up, you lazy pig worshipers and come with me."

Kevin clung to his mat, but Eber yanked him by the ear.

"Ow!" Kevin yelled, following his ear. "I just now went to sleep. It can't be morning yet."

"Morning. Of course it's not morning. It's not yet the middle of the night," Eber growled. "Get up and go with me to find Lamech. He just left his mat and I fear he's up to no good."

Reluctantly Moshe and Kevin stumbled to their feet and followed their master. He carried a lamp with a cover that shed only a thin streak of light at their feet. The boys followed clumsily over the rough ground.

"It's not fair," Kevin muttered. "As hard as we worked all day, we ought to be allowed to sleep through the night. It's just not fair."

Eber held out his hand abruptly and Moshe ran into it. "Hark!" hissed Eber.

The boys listened. The sounds of animals shifting in their sleep told them they were near a flock. Like-wise animal smells wafted to them on the breeze.

"Look," said Eber.

The boys strained their eyes. The moon was only a sliver, but as they stared they were able to make out a shape at the edge of the flock. With an animallike swiftness, the shape moved towards a sheep, sepa-rated it from the flock and hurled it to the ground.

"No," Eber gasped.

The flash of metal glinted in the moonlight and the sheep uttered a bleat in which terror and agony mingled. The dark shape melted into the darkness and the sheep stumbled to its feet. Wide awake now, Moshe stared at the sheep, oblivious of the pounding of running feet and a sudden burst of torchlight off to the distant left of the flock.

"Quick!" came Eber's urgent whisper. "We must not be seen." With rough prods the tanner hurried his slaves away from the commotion behind them. Moshe moved like a person in a nightmare, skin bathed in a cold sweat, his breathing was choked and shallow. As bright as the image of an electric light bulb on your retina after you've shut your eyes, there still burned on his sight the image of the sheep. Moshe had seen plainly, as it stumbled to its feet, that someone had carved a huge piece of meat from the living animal!

# 5

# Plan for Escape

Joshua's men came in the morning.

Moshe recognized the cruel scarred face of the sentry who had captured them and brought them into camp. With him were three other armed men who strode unceremoniously to Eber and began questioning him gruffly about the night's events.

"What do you know about Dathan's sheep?" they demanded.

Eber did not bother to look up from his scraping. "What I know about any sheep," he replied easily. "It has four legs and is easier to skin than a crocodile."

Eber's laughter bawled out and Moshe snorted in amusement. The humorless soldiers glanced his way, scowling.

"You, slave," demanded the one in charge. "What do you know of Dathan's sheep?"

Moshe looked at him blankly. He could sense that the tanner was hanging on his answer, although he never paused in his work or looked in the boy's direction. The investigators seemed to sense it, too. They moved closer to him. Kevin was out of sight and out of earshot on the other side of the tent.

"Sheep?" Moshe said stupidly, looking from one cruel face to the other.

"Sheep, fool!" spat the sentry with the scar and struck Moshe across the face. "The sheep that had a gobbet of flesh cut from it by someone from this stink hole. Dathan's shepherd heard the footsteps going towards this place."

"Wait, Amram," the leader interrupted. "Perhaps the slave does not understand. We must speak slowly for a stranger's ear."

The leader put his face close to Moshe's. Shouting, as if the boy were deaf, he spoke slowly and deliberately.

"The Lord Moses is a fair and generous leader. He rewards those who keep the Law. Tell us who cut the flesh from the living sheep last night. Freedom will be your reward. Do not fear your master Eber there, nor even Korah. No one is above the Lord Moses. What he binds is bound. What he looses is forever loosed. Tell us who cut the flesh from the living sheep last night. That person will die, but freedom will be your reward. You'll be a slave no more."

Moshe's heart leapt. Freedom. If Kevin and he were free of this enslavement to Eber, if they could move about the camp and outside it at will, surely they would be able to find a way back to their own time!

The swarthy face was close to Moshe's. The eyes seemed to bore into his head, looking for the information he wanted. Moshe was aware of the tense figure of Eber scraping at the hide, back and forth, back and forth. With a sudden flash Moshe understood that the tanner's life hung on his answer.

"Sheep?" he said deliberately, ".I know nothing of sheep."

He didn't see where the blow came from, but

Moshe felt himself flying helplessly backwards. He fell against a wooden rack, hitting first his head, then his spine and finally his tailbone, like slow motion, one, two, three. And then he lay there, watching the stars in his head and praying that his back wasn't broken.

"Pig-worshiping jackal," spat the soldier and led his comrades from the tannery.

Moshe lay with his eyes closed, afraid to try to move anything, afraid that he wouldn't be able to. The tanner was bending over him.

"Good work, lad. Old Eber'll not forget," he said, laying a hand gently on Moshe's forehead. "Can you rise, think you?"

Gingerly Moshe moved his body. "I guess so," he said, and allowed the tanner to help him rise. Kevin came around the tent.

"What happened?" Kevin shouted, running up to his friend. "Did he hit you?"

"Eber? No. Soldiers from Joshua. Our old friend the sentry was with them. They wanted to know what we knew about the sheep."

"Aye, lad," said Eber, "go sit by the tent yonder and tell your friend all about it. You need rest just now. These skins won't be going anywhere."

Eber left them and went back to his work. Kevin scowled after him. "Animals!" he spat. "That's what they all are here, filthy, primitive swine. How could anybody do what Lamech did to a living thing? You told them about Lamech, didn't you? I hope they cut him up when they find him!"

With Kevin's help, Moshe limped to the shady side of Eber's tent and sat down carefully.

"Eber didn't tell them about Lamech," he said. "When he didn't tell them anything, they asked me. Said Moses would give me my freedom if I'd tell what I knew about it."

41

Kevin stared at his friend. "Well? Well?" he asked excitedly, "you told them, didn't you? What are we waiting for? Let's get out of here! Let's get back to that place in the desert where we came through that rock formation. It was like a doorway. I'm certain that if we can get back there, we can get back to our own time!"

"I didn't tell them anything," Moshe said.

"What?" The word came out of Kevin's mouth in a scream. His hand shot out and again Moshe felt himself falling to the ground, only this time, as he was sitting, he hadn't so far to fall. He held his arms over his head to ward off the blows that his friend was raining on him.

"You know it was Lamech," Kevin sobbed. "You know it was Lamech. Why didn't you tell them, Moshe? We're slaves. S-l-a-v-e-s. Doesn't that mean anything to you?"

Moshe managed to land a punch of his own, striking Kevin in the belly and stopping the rain of blows. He rolled himself clear.

"I couldn't," Moshe panted. "Can't you guess what they'd do to Eber if they knew he was concealing something?"

"Who cares about Eber?" Kevin howled. "We're trapped in a rotten, barbarian time where people cut up poor dumb animals and make slaves out of human beings. I wouldn't bend a finger to save the life of any one of these filthy animals. You're worried about what might happen to Eber? What do you think Eber cares about you? Have you already forgotten who was kicking us in the ribs last night and calling us pig worshipers? Eber! What about me?" Kevin flung himself down on the ground and buried his head in his arms.

"Look, Kevin," Moshe said, touching his friend gently on the back. "If it will help at all, I think they were just selling me a piece of goods, I don't think they had any intention of taking me to Moses to be set free. They just wanted me to trip up Eber, to see if he was lying."

"Well, he was!" said Kevin. "He was lying. He knows it was Lamech. He suspected as much before last night. If you're so good and honest and such a Christian, how could you lie to protect someone else who was lying?"

"You didn't see them," Moshe tried to explain. "They would have killed him on the spot."

"Fine. Then I'll go find them and tell them what you wouldn't. I'll tell them that Lamech did it and that Eber knew that he did it and that you like being a slave, but that I'd like my freedom, thank you very much ..."

Kevin scrambled to his feet toward the three men who had started down the path to the camp, but the sinewy arms of the tanner who had watched the boys argue closed round him like a vise.

"No, you don't, my lad," Eber grunted.

"You *want* Lamech to die?" asked Moshe in English, so Eber couldn't understand. "Listen, I was just thinking about something I learned in Hebrew school when we studied the Law. Death isn't the right penalty for maiming an animal—in fact, even if someone steals an animal, the Law of Moses says, the penalty is to repay the owner four sheep for every one stolen. You don't kill him. Those guys may have been Joshua's men, but they weren't concerned with what was right. They're just a lynch mob—a bunch of vigilantes making up their own justice."

Kevin flailed violently, but Eber hung on. "It's not that I hold my life so precious that I won't let you tell your tale," Eber said. "A quick slice with a sharp sword is as good a way as any to leave this place of woe.

"No, not death, but the manner of dying is what is on my mind, laddie. I've no wish to die under a shower of rocks: one stone here taking an eye, one there smashing my mouth, another crushing a kneecap. And then I would lie there under the moon, most of the life gone out, but enough left to make me wish for death, waiting for the jackals. No, my boy. Sit you down. If I must, I will truss you up like an Egyptian sacrifice and leave you in the tent day and night till you come round to your friend's way of thinking."

Kevin stopped thrashing. "Let me go," he said between clenched teeth. "I won't do anything."

"Sure, now, are you?" Eber insisted, never relaxing his grip.

"He'll be all right now," Moshe said urgently. "Please let him go, Eber."

Eber let go and Kevin dropped to the ground beside Moshe.

"Animals," Kevin muttered, "any way you cut it, they're a pack of wild animals." He again buried his head in his arms.

"Have there been many stonings?" Moshe asked Eber.

"Not many since we've been here," the tanner replied. "Back in Egypt I saw one. Horrible sight. A woman it was. One of the crowd held her child. A boy about five years old. Just telling of it brings the screams back into my ears."

Eber shuddered and looked closely at Kevin.

"Sure you'll not be running off to Joshua as soon as my back's turned?" he demanded.

"Sure," Kevin mumbled without lifting his head.

Eber turned to Moshe. "Rest until mealtime," he said. "If Lamech hasn't come back after the midday rest, I'll show you how to start the new skins that

Aaron sent. Keep a sharp eye on your friend. When stones begin to fly, they don't know the difference between master and man. If Lamech is found out and it's learned that I shielded him, it's not likely they'll stone me and spare my two slaves."

Eber left them.

The boys sat in silence.

For the first time since realizing that he and Kevin were in another time, Moshe felt fingers of fear crawl along the back of his neck. Stoning. Reading of it in the Bible, Moshe had shuddered at the thought of such a barbaric form of execution, shuddered and gone on, secure in the knowledge that it was a practice that belonged to antiquity; something barbaric and extinct, like human sacrifice; outside his world, no part of his culture. Now the extinct custom walked his imagination like a Frankenstein's monster, rising suddenly in his own house instead of being safely imprisoned in a book or on a movie screen. Stoning. Stephen lifting his eyes to heaven as the stones flew and Saul held the coats of the killers.

"Kevin, we've got to get away from here! Your idea about the doorway in the desert. It might not work, but it's the best hope we have. We'll watch our chance. With Lamech gone, Eber might send us into the desert on an errand."

The sun passed its zenith. Rest was over and Eber summoned them to their work. Lamech had not yet come back. Moshe moved slowly, painfully, like an old man with an ache in every joint.

"It will pass, lad," Eber encouraged him. "Work is best, you know. Work heals most things."

Little conversation passed between them over work or over supper. Now Eber, now Kevin, now Moshe would pause at what he was doing, glance at the horizon, shrug and go back to the scraping or skinning or the eating. Once, just at sunset as the sun stood poised over the horizon, Moshe glanced in the direction of Korah's tents. "Would you look at that!"

Eber and Kevin followed his gaze.

Outlined against the red of the setting sun stood the robed figure of a man, arms upraised, golden ornaments flashing and glinting electrically in the last vivid rays of the sun. Clouds of smoke swirled about his figure, catching the crimson and purple hues of the sunset. Then, as if summoned, the sun dropped below the horizon and the man disappeared into the sudden absence of light.

"What was that all about, Eber?" Moshe asked. "Was that—was that Moses?"

"Moses!" Eber snorted. "The one true God show mercy on you, boy! Moses would have knocked him down with his staff if he'd been looking on as we were. Yonder was Korah, saying his evening prayers with his precious censer and robes and all that Egyptian truck. Moses has forbidden it. I wonder that Korah would be so open in it. Lamech has perhaps touched off more mischief than we know."

Moshe recalled the blue-robed figure of Korah on the day they had entered the camp. Chief of the golden ornaments had been the winged orb. He recalled trying to place the symbol, golden wings on a golden ball. Now it came to him.

"It's the sun disk!" he exclaimed. "That winged symbol Korah wears and has in his tent is the Egyptian symbol for the sun."

"Of course!" breathed Kevin, "now it's starting to make some sense."

Moshe looked wide-eyed at Eber. "Is Korah a sun worshiper?"

Eber looked around nervously. "He'd better not be," Eber said, lowering his voice. "He says he is not, says the winged thing is just a respectful symbol of the one God whose name no man may speak. I notice he takes care to see that it's covered up when he goes to the Tent of Meeting. He knows what Moses would do, I'll be bound."

Eber spat into the fire and stretched. "Time for sleep, lads. I'll sleep in Lamech's spot tonight."

Moshe and Kevin went to their mats inside the tent and waited until the tanner's breathing was even.

"Moshe? Are you awake?"

"Yes."

Moshe could hear an excitement and banter in his friend's voice that had been absent since their capture. It was the tone he used when he thought he was about to demolish a cherished Christian belief, like contending that the Star of Bethlehem was an extinct supernova.

"Have you ever read anything about Akhenaten?" Kevin whispered.

Moshe pondered. "Yes," he said finally. "He was a pharaoh who lived before the time of Moses. He started out as Amenhotep IV, but changed his name."

"That's not all he changed," Kevin said. "He changed the religion of Egypt, or at least tried. Akhenaten was the first monotheist. He tried to get the Egyptians to worship one god instead of the dozens they had."

"Well, what happened?" Moshe asked, wishing he could remember more of what he had read about the unusual pharaoh. "Why did the Egyptians go on worshiping Ra and Horus and Isis and all the others right up to the time of Christ?"

"Akhenaten died, that's what happened. He didn't have anyone to carry on his ideas. While he reigned he kicked out the priests of Amon—that's why he changed his name from AMENhotep to AkhenATEN. Amon was the god they worshiped at

Thebes and Aten was a name for the sun. Akhenaten kicked out the priests of Amon, scratched out the words Amon and Amen on all the monuments of his father, built new temples, plastered the winged sun disk all over the place, and generally made everybody mad. When he died, the priests of Amon went around scratching out all the Atens and putting back the Amens. All of Akhenaten's work was overturned, thrown out, forgotten by everyone except—get this, Moshe—except for the Children of Israel!"

Moshe heard the triumph in Kevin's voice, but he didn't understand what his friend was trying to prove.

"I don't get it," said Moshe.

"It's as plain as Korah worshiping the sunset, Moshe. Moses and his talks with the burning bush and all that other stuff is just a variation of Akhenaten's teachings about the Aten. The Hebrews in the wilderness are just runaway Egyptian slaves who brought out some Egyptian religious ideas. They're just a bunch of sun worshipers!"

Kevin lay back on his mat and waited for Moshe to ponder what he had said.

Moshe did ponder. He recalled now having read a prayer written by the pharaoh Akhenaten. It was a song of praise to the sun that warmed and gave life to all, that shone on all countries, thus making all men brothers. His father had told him that some nonbelievers pointed to this hymn as evidence that monotheism had not begun with the Jews. "There's only one catch to your theory," Moshe finally said.

"What?" Kevin demanded. "It's a beautiful theory, a flawless theory. Moses was probably a young man when Akhenaten died. He grew up in a royal household. He would have heard about the old pharaoh's views. The idea of one god appealed to him. He thought it over for years."

"No," said Moshe, "it won't hold water. The Hebrews knew about the one God *before* they went to Egypt. And Eber told us that Moses would knock Korah down if he saw him praying to the sun. Korah may be a closet sun worshiper, but Moses serves God. The only God. Akhenaten was close to the truth, but he couldn't get beyond the idea of a visible god. He wasn't really the first monotheist, as you called him. Akhenaten was just a pagan who tried to set up the sun as the only thing to be worshiped. He never saw behind the sun to where God is."

"Have it your way," Kevin grumbled. "Some people can't see the truth when it sits on them."

"How true," retorted Moshe and rolled over to sleep.

Sleep, however, was long in coming. Moshe stared into the darkness of the tent, his mind still in motion from his exchange with his friend. All their religious discussions ended the same way. Kevin believed in the invisible world of atoms, sound waves, and even things like ESP, but the idea of a creator with a continuing interest in his creation was an offense to him.

Moshe prayed, for himself, for Kevin, and for poor, unhappy Eber. At last he fell into an unrestful sleep full of dreams....

First he was standing in the desert, outside the camp. He was all alone and terrified. He turned this way and that, like an animal looking for a way to escape his hunters. His ears throbbed with a distant sound that became louder and louder. The sound struck terror into him.

As it grew louder, he recognized it as the sound of many voices, men and women, even the shrill shouts of children. Suddenly he could see them, swarms of people from the camp, coming over a little rise in streams, like the rats swarming out of the houses of Hamelin town.

The voices were clearer now, all were shouting the same chant. "Stone him! Stone him! Stone him!"

Moshe's tongue was dry; his heart was pounding; he tried to shout for help, but his lips and tongue could not form the words. The people stooped as they came towards him, scooping up stones. The front rank burst into a trot, then a run, and the first stones were hurled. Moshe shut his eyes and threw up his hands to protect his head. He heard some of the stones whiz past him and then heard one strike flesh. He knew with the certainty one has in dreams that the stone had struck a living body, yet he knew, that he had not felt it.

Next he saw a man standing between him and the mob. He was not dressed like the others and his beard was golden. He stood tall and broad-shouldered in the sunlight, a hero like Roland or Siegfried. He took the stones aimed at Moshe. Here and there streaks of blood stained his princely cloth-ing, but he did not flinch. He turned around and Moshe gazed gratefully into his eyes. They were bright and compelling and filled with the kind of love he sometimes saw in the eyes of his parents when they were feeling particularly proud of him. He looked beyond the man to the mob and saw the angry stoners flailing their arms futilely as they faded like phantoms into the desert air. The man, the Prince, reached out his hand and touched Moshe on the forehead. Immediately all the terror flowed out of him and in its place came a calm sense of peace and safety. Moshe slipped into a restful sleep, secure in the knowledge of who his cham-pion was.

# 6

# Doorway to Nowhere

The yapping of the dog pack preceded two men and a small boy into Eber's domain.

Lamech still wasn't back, but the evidence of his savage nocturnal attack was in the hands of one of the men. Inexperienced as he was, Moshe knew that a fresh hide was never cut in such a way.

"Morning, Abiram, morning, Zimran," Eber said shortly. He did not greet the boy but stared at him for a long moment before going back to his work.

"Dathan wants this tanned," growled the man called Abiram. "Moses said we had to go ahead and have it killed. A lot Moses knows about livestock. That sheep could have lived and grown more meat. Moses is a softy about animals. Won't let them suffer a little."

Abiram spat, splattering Kevin who lurched away furiously. The little boy with Abiram laughed loudly.

"I'll hear nothing against the Lord Moses in my tents!" Eber thundered suddenly. "He is our leader and he is the messenger of the God of Israel!"

Moshe stared at the tanner. In their conversations over work and over meals, he had come to believe that Eber did not believe much of anything when it came to religious matters. Was it fear, he wondered, or something else, that had the man so wound up?

"Listen to him rage," said Abiram, "as if he didn't know who wielded the knife that left the hole in this hide."

"I know that this was not the hand," Eber retorted passionately, brandishing his right hand at them. "Leave it here and begone. I must cure the hides of all, but I don't have to listen to the likes of you while I work!"

"Don't fret yourself, tanner," said Abiram. "We'll keep our opinions to ourselves, but we'll wait to see that we get back what we brought. We want to see you mark it."

Moshe watched Abiram and Zimran follow Eber to another work area. He wondered what additional mark was needed for a hide that had a giant hole in it.

Abiram's boy, who was about four, squatted and picked up some small stones to cast at a puppy that had left the pack and was trying to make friends with him. First the boy cast them wide, hitting only the ground, but then, in rapid succession, he struck the animal sharply on the side, on the nose, and in the left eye. It fled yelping back to the pack while the child laughed delightedly. The men looked over.

"Good aim, Seth," Abiram roared with approval. "You'll keep the lion from the fold when we get to the Land of Promise."

"If we get to the Land of Promise" said Zimran, contemptuously.

"Beware what you say," mocked Abiram, feigning a fearful crouch, "Eber will not like such talk."

The child settled down to some other activity in the dust. Moshe went closer to see what he was doing. He was pulling the legs off a dung beetle, one leg at a time, setting the insect back on the ground to see if it could still crawl, then pulling off the next.

"You young devil!" Moshe exclaimed, moving quickly to crush the beetle and end its torment.

Startled, the child ran screaming to Abiram who whirled angrily and looked accusingly at Moshe.

"What did the slave do to you?" he demanded.

"He stepped on my beetle!" the boy complained, weeping loudly.

"He was tormenting the poor creature," said Moshe. "He was pulling its legs off. I ended its suffering."

Abiram exploded in laughter and the boy's face turned to smiles in the midst of tears.

"A beetle!" he exclaimed. "The slave's offended by a boy's innocent play with a beetle! You should have seen what he did to the kitten that scratched him yestermorn. It will never scratch as a cat, I can tell you!"

Placing his hand proudly on the boy's shoulder, Abiram walked away, calling over his shoulder.

"He's marked it right enough. Let's be going."

"What did he do to the kitten?" Moshe reluctantly asked Zimran.

"Pulled its little claws out one by one, like he done with the beetle's legs," said Zimran. "Getting to be just like Abiram," he said loudly, as if he wished to be sure that Eber heard, "a son to be proud of."

The dogs saw the strangers off with their usual clamor and as soon as it died down, Eber went behind the tent and returned immediately with

Lamech. Moshe thought he understood now why the tanner had been eager to get rid of Abiram and Zimran.

"It doesn't matter who knows I'm back," Lamech said. "No one can prove anything against me. None of Dathan's household would want to."

"Then why were his men Abiram and Zimran so particular about the marking?" Eber demanded. "They're up to no good. Something is going on. Korah was praying with incense in plain sight last night and now Dathan is insisting on a hide with a hole in it being specially marked. Why would he do that if he wasn't expecting me to be handling some more hides with untimely holes in them?

"You two!" Eber motioned to Moshe and Kevin. "I want you to go into the desert with Lamech for jackal dung. We're almost out and I need more than one man can carry. Each of you take a basket and don't come back until they're full."

Lamech shrugged and took a basket. Moshe and Kevin exchanged excited glances. Here was their chance to go into the desert. Moshe looked at Lamech. The big man seemed rested and contented. He decided to take a chance.

"Is there any special place you go, Lamech?" he asked.

Lamech shook his head. "Just out there. If I see jackal tracks, I follow them until I find one of their resting places."

Moshe tried to sound casual.

"I noticed a place, near where we spent the night, before we were brought into the camp—must have been twenty jackals holed up there once. There's enough stuff in that one spot to fill six baskets like these."

Moshe pretended to be interested in his basket, but glanced furtively at Lamech. He was scratching his shaggy head thoughtfully. "How far?" he grunted.

"Not more than a mile. Maybe less."

"Show me."

Moshe's heart leapt joyfully. *Please let us get there,* he prayed silently. *Please let us get to the doorway.*

"Don't come back before the midday rest," Eber said. He looked steadily at Kevin.

"I look for Joshua's men to come round before midday if they come again looking for answers."

Lamech placed a huge paw on Kevin's shoulder.

"Think you this one might want to give some answers?" He squeezed his fingers round Kevin's neck.

"Quit it, Lamech," Eber barked, and Lamech dropped his hand.

"Do not abuse them," Eber warned him. "They must answer to me or to Korah. And you, slaves. You mind Lamech and don't try anything foolish. If you disobey him, I will punish you. If I'm not here, he will take you to Korah. And let me tell you that Korah is not so merciful a man as I. Go now."

Lamech strode ahead in long, ground-eating strides while Moshe and Kevin, still unused to the rough rudimentary sandals, stumbled after him awkwardly, clutching their collecting baskets.

Occasionally the sullen tanner would stop in his tracks, back toward them, and wait until he heard them clamber to within a yard or so and then resume walking, never once looking back at them.

Desperately the boys scanned the empty desolate landscape looking for some familiar landmark, some outcropping, some pile of rocks that they could remember from their long walk into the camp of Moses.

When they had been walking for about twenty

minutes, Moshe stopped and stared into the distance. It was a feeling more than anything he saw, but he was certain that the stone archway was somewhere to the east of the way they were walking.

"Over there!" he shouted to Lamech who had again paused. "Over there, many jackals, many droppings."

Lamech glanced back at Moshe. He shrugged and turned in the direction Moshe was pointing.

"Are you sure?" Kevin asked, his breath coming short from exertion and excitement. "I can't recognize any of this. It all looks alike whichever way I turn."

Moshe shook his head. "I don't know for sure," he said, "but I feel like—almost like—something is drawing me in that direction."

The boys quickened their steps and fell in behind Lamech, alternately walking and jogging to keep up. The sun was almost directly in their eyes and they felt light-headed. Lamech was beginning to show signs of impatience. Now when he stopped he waited until they were right behind him. Then he whirled and struck them both at once with his arm, across their faces.

"There had better be jackals," he said ominously, "and soon."

The unexpectedness of the blow more than its force sent both boys to the ground in a heap under their baskets. They helped each other up and stood still to catch their breaths.

Then Moshe saw it. "Look over there. It's the arch. It's the formation we came through."

They began to run towards Lamech, but when they came up even with him, he grabbed them each by the neck and held them.

"You will not run away," he said and squeezed his thick fingers into their necks.

"We're not trying to run away," Kevin choked. "We're just trying to get to those rocks over there. It's like a big doorway, see. That's the place where we saw the jackal stuff. Honest, we're just trying to get there to fill our baskets."

Lamech grunted and released their necks.

"Slow," he said.

Slowly, hearts pounding, the boys moved towards the rock formation, which they were certain was a doorway that would lead them back into their own time. About forty yards from it, they came to an area thickly littered with the droppings they were supposed to be looking for. With a grunt of satisfaction Lamech threw his own basket at the boys and seated himself comfortably in the shade of a rock.

"Plenty here," he growled. "Fill all the baskets."

Moshe and Kevin set to work reluctantly.

"We'll never get to the doorway," Kevin hissed.

"Let's work in that direction," Moshe whispered. "Lamech's eyes are closed. Maybe he'll doze off and we can get that far before he wakes up."

Breathing hard, the boys picked up as little as possible, moving always toward the stone doorway. They still had about twenty yards to go when Lamech shouted for them to come back.

"Run for it!" barked Moshe.

Dropping their baskets the boys sprinted for the formation. Above the pounding of their hearts, they could hear the thudding and flapping of Lamech's heavy sandaled feet.

Lungs bursting, Moshe flung himself through the formation, Kevin at his heels. Clinging to each other they looked back through the doorway, waiting, tensed in every muscle and nerve, waiting for the light and the roaring to encompass them.

The desert air remained unaltered. The sounds in their ears were the usual desert noises and the angry thud of Lamech's feet as he came closer. The stone arch stood unchanged above them. There was no magic in it, and they weren't going anywhere.

# 7
# Ten Whiplashes

Lamech's fingers closed around their necks with a force that made their eyes start from their heads.

"Pig-worshiping slaves!" he spat, shaking them like rats. "It would give me much pleasure to tear you to pieces and leave your parts for the jackals."

With another shake he flung them from him, back through the archway. "Fill your baskets, offal," he commanded. "If you belonged to Dathan and not to Korah, I could do as I would and fear no displeasure."

Moshe was chilled by the look in the tanner's eyes. Despite his words, there was no disappointment there, only a kind of savage glee.

"Lord Korah is a bloody man," Lamech said with fierce satisfaction. "You will be fortunate if all he does is bore your ears as runaways."

Moshe fingered his earlobe and shivered. The two boys grabbed their baskets and started collecting jackal dung.

When the baskets were full, Lamech drove his

slaves before him to the tanning yard. Eber was not there.

Lamech grunted with what looked like pleasure. "I take you to Lord Korah."

Moshe felt his flesh crawl. If only they would meet Eber on the way. Eber was rough, but he did not seem to share the cruelty of some of the other ancient Hebrews they had encountered so far.

Lamech kicked at a stack of skins. "Korah's," he said. "They are ready. Carry them."

Kevin and Moshe split the load, but even half a stack was extremely heavy and their arms and backs ached horribly by the time they reached Korah's tent.

"There," Lamech pointed and the boys dropped the skins behind the tent. Then Lamech led them round to the entrance and called. "Lord Korah, justice from Lord Korah!"

There was a movement inside and then a head and shoulders pushed past the hangings to reveal not Korah but the handsome young man who had been there on the day Kevin and Moshe had had their feet washed.

"I speak for Korah in his absence," said the young man. "What justice is required?"

"These slaves of the Lord Korah attempted to run away," Lamech said. "They must be punished. Eber is away from home so I brought them here."

"Leave them with me," the young man commanded. "When my father returns, he will deal with them."

"Twenty lashes at least," Lamech said urgently, "and boring of the ears with the hot awl."

"Go," said the young man. "My father will decide the punishment."

"I will wait," said Lamech, bowing and preparing to sit down outside the tent.

The young man fixed him with blazing eyes. "I speak for my father," he said. "You may go. The slaves will be dealt with."

Lamech dropped his gaze, bowed and went away.

"Enter," said the man, and Kevin and Moshe went into the tent.

The air inside was heavy with incense. The young man sat on a cushion and motioned to the boys to be seated before him.

"I am Akohath," he said. "I am second son to Lord Korah. He has gone to the tent of meeting but will be back before sundown. I remember you. You are the pig worshipers my father sent to Eber."

Moshe studied the young man's face. His first impression returned more strongly than before. The lines around the mouth were firm, but not cruel. The eyes were clear and honest. He searched for words that would explain their bizarre situation and would enlist Akohath's sympathies without making him think they were crazy.

"My lord Akohath," he began carefully. "My friend and I are not pig worshipers. We ... I, worship the one true God, him whom you worship. In our country the pig is not, is just a," Moshe paused in some confusion. Kevin had showed him motion pictures of a football game in Arkansas. The hog symbol had been everywhere, on neckties, shirts, shoes, watches, cars, some people had even been wearing grotesque plastic helmets shaped like a pig's face, which made them look like tribal witch doctors dressed for a ritual. How did one explain the difference between a mascot and a totem animal to a man of ancient times to whom everything had some kind of religious significance?

"It is just a clothing decoration," Moshe finished lamely, "kind of like stripes or circles."

Akohath glanced sharply at one of the sun disks that decorated his father's tent and Moshe regretted instantly that he had mentioned circles. To Akohath a circle was not mere decoration for clothing. It was the symbol for the Egyptian deity Aten.

"It is difficult for me to understand," said Akohath, "why one would wish to wear the picture of a pig on one's clothing if it had no religious significance."

Moshe nodded a little hysterically. "This is because with your people such things are religious symbols. In our country all manner of animals, birds and fish and beasts are used to decorate clothing."

"And flowers," offered Kevin, understanding enough of the conversation to be able to join in, "and fruit. My little sister has a nightgown that has monkeys and bananas all over it."

Akohath looked quizzically from Kevin to Moshe. Kevin had been unable to think of the Hebrew words for nightgown, monkeys, or bananas and had used the English words.

Akohath spoke gravely. "Your native tongue is not Egyptian nor any of the Canaanite tongues that I have heard. What are your names?"

Moshe thought quickly. Although Hebrew in form, his name was the same as that of Moses. To avoid the complications of having to explain, he decided to give his last name.

"My name is Drummond," he said. "My friend's name is Kevin."

Akohath repeated the names carefully.

"I have heard these names," he said. "If you are spies, what nation are you?"

"We are not spies, Lord Akohath," Moshe said. "Our language is called English. It is not a language spoken by anyone you will meet as long as you live. I cannot explain how my friend and I came to be in your camp. I cannot tell you because I do not know. I only know that we were in our own country and then we were here. We do not wish to be here. We wish to return to our own place, but we do not know how to get there."

"Did you try to run away from Lamech?"

"Yes," said Moshe, "but we are not slaves! At least we weren't until we got here. Can it really be the custom of your people to enslave free men?"

Akohath shook his head, frowning. "It is not our custom to do so," he said. "Custom was broken when you were not taken to Moses and the elders when you were first discovered." Akohath sighed. "Now that you have been turned over to Eber, your position is not so clear."

Moshe could sense that Akohath was not in agreement with what his father had done, but would not openly criticize him.

"Please, Lord Akohath," said Moshe. "We beg justice at your hands. Is there any way you can help us?"

As Akohath pondered the question, the tent hangings stirred and the splendid form of Korah entered.

"What are these?" Korah demanded, seeing the slaves crouched before his son.

Akohath rose respectfully and bowed slightly to his father. "Eber's man, Lamech, brought them here, my lord. He says that they failed to obey."

Moshe heard with relief that Akohath chose not to use the term "run away."

Korah put his head close to theirs and recognition dawned in his eyes. He spat. "Pah! The pig worshipers! Call for the sandal maker. Tell him to heat his awl. We bore the ears of disobedient slaves!"

Akohath put out his hand to his father. "My lord, it is their first offense. Are we not taught to show mercy to our slaves, even to the third offense?"

Korah shrugged angrily. "First Moses, now you, my son? In Egypt I was a teacher, now am I to be taught by a sheepherder and a younger son?"

Korah's words were angry, but Moshe sensed a pulling back, a reluctance to insist on his will. Akohath, too, sensed a change in his father's will. "Was there much talk at the meeting, father?"

"Much talk and nothing done, as usual. Yet the strength is still with Moses and Aaron. We must bring our animals to Aaron for offerings. We must show mercy to our slaves even to the third offense."

Sarcasm, Moshe noticed, sounded about the same in ancient Hebrew as it did in English.

Korah shrugged again and turned away.

"Very well," he said to his son. "You needn't bore their ears this time. But see that they get a good whipping. Ten lashes each should teach them obedience."

Akohath bowed and motioned the boys to precede him out of the tent.

Korah called after him. "Have Guerin peg them just behind the tent," he said. "It will do me good to hear their cries. I can pretend they are ... two others I'll not name."

Guerin turned out to be one of the two slaves who had taken Moshe and Kevin to the tanner. He came running with pegs, a mallet, and a look of anticipation.

"Lie down," said Akohath.

Reluctantly, Moshe and Kevin lay facedown in the dirt beside the stack of hides they had brought. Guerin roughly tied their hands and feet to the pegs when he had driven them into the hard ground. He tied the leather thongs so tightly that they bit into the flesh of their wrists and ankles.

"Shall I lay on the lashes, Lord Akohath?" the slave asked eagerly.

"No, Guerin," said Akohath, "I'll do it. Give me the whip and go."

"Please, my lord," said Guerin, disappointment heavy in his voice, "may I not watch?"

"Go," Akohath repeated, and Moshe and Kevin could hear the slave's feet drag reluctantly away.

Clearly, Moshe thought, Akohath did not intend to harm them and had sent the slave away so there would be no witness.

"Courage," said Akohath kindly, and brought the whip down whistling through the air.

Surprise mingled with searing pain as the lash cut into the flesh of his bare back and Moshe's scream split the air.

"One!" said Akohath.

# 8

# The Tent of Akohath

The pain of the whiplash was unlike anything Moshe had ever felt. No sunburn, no scrape or cut or accidentally broken bone of his thirteen years of existence could compare to the searing slash of the whip that had made a path in the flesh of his back.

Added to the pain was the sense of betrayal because the blow had come from one he had thought to be his friend.

Akohath's voice came close to his ear.

"Continue to cry out," he said softly. "I will spare you as much as I can."

Again the whip whizzed through the air and this time it was Kevin's scream that split the air.

Again Akohath shouted, "One!"

Moshe gritted his teeth. He was going to whip them in turn. He braced himself for the second blow, but this time Akohath brought the lash down on the stack of tanned hides that lay nearby.

"Scream!" hissed Akohath.

Moshe screamed.

"Two!" Akohath shouted.

Again and again Akohath brought the whip down on the stack of hides and the boys cried out.

After the fifth pair of strokes, Akohath leaned down and whispered urgently. "You've got to cry out more loudly than that," he hissed. "Have you forgotten the pain so quickly?"

The next time the lash descended it cut across Moshe's back and a genuine scream again split the air.

"Six!" counted Akohath, as he brought the lash down on Kevin's back. Kevin howled.

"Remember the pain," Akohath whispered. "My father is no fool. I have seen him draw screams from grown men to the fiftieth stroke!"

Moshe and Kevin needed no more reminders. They both cried out convincingly and Akohath finished the count of ten without touching them again.

Akohath threw down the whip and went back into his father's tent. Moshe and Kevin could hear their voices and then footsteps coming back.

"My father has given me leave to take you to my own tent until you recover," said Akohath, leaning over them and untying the thongs that bound them to the pegs. "His mind is much on matters that were discussed at the tent of meeting today."

Painfully the boys got to their feet. Moshe could not hold back a groan. His back burned like fire. He hated to think what it would feel like had Akohath administered all ten lashes.

With Korah's son supporting them, the boys managed to walk to Akohath's tent. Inside it was cool and scented with spices. Akohath helped them lie down on their stomachs. Then they were aware of a woman's cool gentle hands on their backs.

"This may hurt a little, but first it must be cleaned."

The voice was pleasant and sympathetic. The hands were quick, but even so the touch of water made the boys cry out.

"Now the salve," said the voice, soothingly, while the hands gently patted away the water. "The salve will not hurt, there."

Moshe's worn-out nerves began to relax as the salve touched his wounds. A medicinal scent came to his nostrils. A pleasant warmth spread over the lash marks and he expelled a deep sigh of relief.

"Thank you," he murmured to the unseen woman. "Thanks."

"Sleep now," said the woman. "Sleep heals most hurts."

When Moshe woke the next morning he could feel a dull smarting and was very thirsty. He sat up and looked around the tent.

Kevin was leaning against some cushions, sipping something from an earthen bowl.

Two women were placing dishes on a low table. They looked towards them and he could see that one was just a girl. The woman spoke. "Good! Just in time to join us for the evening meal. How is your back? I put ointment on it when you fell asleep."

"Much better," Moshe said. "You did a good job."

Gingerly Moshe contorted his arm to feel the cuts on his back. They felt sticky. He sniffed his finger, then touched his tongue to it. The salve tasted sweet, like honey.

"There really wasn't much to do," offered the girl with a toss of her head. "You can't have had more than two lashes apiece. You should have seen poor Guerin's back that time that Grandfather caught him ..."

"Hold your tongue, Miriam," snapped the older woman. "Two lashes or twenty, it tears the flesh and gives great pain. Who are you to compare sufferings you never bore yourself?"

Miriam bit her lip and went back to laying out the meal.

Kevin came over to sit beside Moshe. "Want a sip?" he asked, offering the bowl.

Moshe sipped. It was spiced and hot and sent a pleasant warmth through his body.

"You'll never guess what they put on our backs," he said. "Honey!"

Kevin grunted. "I know," he said. "It beats me how they figured out that kind of thing in ancient times."

"What do you mean?" Moshe asked.

"Honey," said Kevin. "It's antibacterial. It kills bacteria by drawing water out of their cells."

Akohath pushed through the tent flap and smiled at the boys. "How are the backs? Much better, I expect. My wife Tamar is a great healer and my daughter Miriam is not far behind. Are you able to sit with us?"

Moshe and Kevin joined the family at the low table. Akohath asked the blessing, and then Tamar and Miriam served them a simple meal of coarse bread, cheese, and goat's milk.

"The salve helped a lot," said Moshe. "I don't know that I could have lived through ten strokes with that whip."

Akohath smiled grimly.

"You could live through ten," he said with certainty. "I am sorry that I had to strike you even twice, but if my father had come out it would have gone much worse for you."

Kevin studied Akohath's face as if looking for something. "I don't want you to think that I don't appreciate your giving us only two lashes," he said. "I wish you hadn't given us any. But I'm wondering why you didn't give us the full ten. Your father told you to do it. I know that your Law commands you to

69

obey your father."

Akohath raised his eyebrows. "How is it you know of our commandments?" he asked. "I would not have expected Eber to have given you instruction in anything other than tanning."

Moshe spoke quickly. "We have asked many things in the evening," he said. "Eber has told us much of your ways."

"I see," said Akohath. "Kevin's remark is just. The Law commands me to honor my father. But it also commands me to love my neighbor as myself. I would not give my own body to the whip, so how can I willingly bring the lash down on the back of my neighbor? Yet my father commands me. What do I do? I give two lashes instead of ten. Have I sinned by giving the two lashes? Or have I sinned by not giving ten? It is a hard question."

Kevin looked at Akohath with respect.

"You are the first of your people I've met," he said, "who seems to worry very much about obeying the Law, especially the part about treating strangers decently."

"Old habits are difficult to change," said Akohath. "A man may know what is right and still not do it. And there are many among us who are not convinced in their minds that Moses speaks for God in everything."

"You've got to admit," said Kevin, thinking of the lists and lists of rules in Leviticus, "Moses has given you an awful lot of *do's* and *don't's* to keep straight."

"No," said Akohath, "the heart of the Law is simple enough for a child to learn: to love the Lord God who took us out of Egypt—to have no idols—to honor our parents—to provide for the poor among us—to protect the stranger—and to require just treatment under the Law for everyone, rich or poor, highborn or lowborn."

"You make it sound so simple," said Moshe.

"Yes," said Akohath. "It is simple to one who has been brought up in it and has never known any other law. But to our elders, who grew up in Egypt, it is a burden and a stumbling block. To my father, a prayer to the Lord and obedience to the Law is not enough. His mind is so set in the complicated form of worship he grew up with, he says he cannot worship God under the covenant we received at Sinai."

"At least your father seems to be concerned with spiritual things," said Kevin, "but I can't think Abiram or that sentry who brought us in ever thinks of such things."

"Dathan and Abiram rebel over other things," Akohath agreed. "The idea of justice for all the people and compassion for beasts is more offensive to them than slavery. They cannot abide a law that forbids men to make victims of others."

"I guess you'll just have to stay in the wilderness until the old ideas die out with the old folks," said Moshe, knowing that that was what God had finally required of the contentious people he had brought out of Egypt.

"Perhaps," Akohath nodded. "Yes." he said, "but even when that day comes, I wonder if we dare leave the wilderness to settle in the Land of Canaan."

"But God has promised!" exclaimed Miriam. "He has promised to give us the land."

"Yes, of course, and he keeps his promises. I spoke only from my own fears. I fear what will happen when this people settles down among the inhabitants of the land," said Akohath. "They will have their own ways."

"You'll have to teach them," said Moshe. "By then all your people will have the Law in their hearts so you will all be teachers. Wherever any of you settle, you will spread God's Word."

"I would like to believe that that is the way it will be," Akohath said earnestly. "But I have seen travelers return from strange lands. The longer they stay, the more they discard their ways. They come back dressed like the natives of the land they have visited, speaking with the accents of the stranger's speech, wearing ornaments bought in their bazaars, cooking their foods, thinking their ideas."

"But," protested Moshe, "your people will have the truth. The ones who are there will have to listen, will have to be changed by it."

"May it be as you say, Drummond," said Akohath. "But I do fear the power that is in numbers, the power that is in the established ways of a native people. I fear that this evil may work even on God's people to take them in and make them over until, like a traveler from a far country, they wear the dress of their hosts."

Tamar took her husband's hand in hers. "In every generation," she said, "there are the weak, the thoughtless, the ones who care more for the words of men than of God. But always there are the true-hearted ones, the men like you, my husband, who carry God's Word in their hearts and when others forget, cry out to remind them. God will never leave us without our prophets," she said confidently.

Akohath sat up suddenly. "Do not name me with the prophets!" he exclaimed in great consternation. "Even this stranger rebukes me for failing to obey the commandment to honor my father!"

"Moses has taught us that God is good," said Tamar. "Surely a God who is good sees into the heart and sifts a man's intentions from his deeds. You withheld the lash because of the command to love your neighbor."

Akohath shook his head. "Moses has also taught

us that God is just," he said, "surely a God who is just will reward or punish a man for what he does and not for what he intends to do."

Akohath stared gloomily at the table. Tamar continued to hold his hand. No one else felt like speaking. At last his expression began to clear a little. "My father erred when he sent you to Eber and not to Moses," he said. "And I was wrong to keep silent. The Law is clear. We must not afflict a stranger for we were strangers in the land of Egypt. Tomorrow I will take you before the elders at the tent of meeting," he said. "You did not come to us as purchased slaves, so a judgment must be made before the assembly."

He waved at the mats where the boys had rested after the whipping. "You will sleep here tonight," he said. "I will go now and tell Eber what I intend to do." With a firm step, Akohath swept out of the tent. Miriam and her mother began to clear away the supper things.

"We're going to see Moses!" Moshe was almost dizzy with excitement.

"Yeah," said Kevin, "but unless he can hit a rock with his staff and make us a doorway to the twentieth century, so what?"

"You don't fool me," said Moshe. "You're just as excited as I am!"

Long after the even breathing of Akohath and his family filled the silence of the tent that night, Moshe and Kevin tossed on their cushions, eyes wide open in the darkness.

# 9
# Rebellion in the Camp

"Wake up!" Akohath urged, shaking the boys by the shoulders. "We must get there early if we hope to speak to Moses or even to one of the judges he has appointed."

Moshe and Kevin needed no urging. They were on their feet in a second, scuffing on their sandals, and following Akohath out of the tent.

"It sure is an advantage sleeping in your clothes," Kevin observed as they lengthened their steps to keep up with Akohath.

"It's not so bad when all you have is a loincloth like us," agreed Moshe, "but it hasn't done much for *their* appearance."

He nodded towards a knot of people standing outside a tent, two men and three women, all wearing rumpled, dirty tunics that went over one shoulder and came down to their knees.

"Not too nifty," Kevin agreed, "but think of the time it saves."

Akohath strode ahead of them, surely and rapidly, weaving in and out between tents and knots of people. Here and there women squatted over what looked like large, overturned flowerpots.

"Look!" Moshe exclaimed as he realized what they were. "Ovens! They're baking the day's bread in clay ovens. Wouldn't my mom just love it if I could bring her back one of those all in one piece!"

Kevin could never resist the obvious. "She'll love it more if you can manage to get yourself back in one piece," he said.

The press of people increased, and Moshe and Kevin had to concentrate on keeping up with Akohath. He led them to an area where curtains were arranged along the sides of a square.

In the midst of the square were small groups of people standing around.

Moshe nudged Kevin. "Have you noticed that there aren't any women or babies here? Just men."

"Yeah. And almost everyone is leading a sheep or goat—except that guy over there with the birds."

Most of the people were dressed like Moshe and Kevin, in loincloths, or like the group they had seen earlier, in crumpled tunics.

"Not what you'd call a very prosperous looking bunch," observed Kevin. "Isn't there something in Exodus about all the gold and jewelry they took out of Egypt?"

"They must have used it all on the ark and the Tabernacle," said Moshe. He looked around the square trying to get a glimpse of the richly decorated tent where he expected to find the Ark of the Covenant. Then he looked at the curtains surrounding this square. The crowd within the fabric walls was growing thicker all the time and all he could see were backs and shoulders.

"Stand close to me," Akohath told them. "I am looking for Caleb. He will help us get close to the tent of Moses so we'll have a better chance of being heard. There he is. Caleb! What news?"

A good-looking young man a little taller than Akohath elbowed his way towards them. He wore a striped red, green, and blue tunic and carried a dagger thrust into his broad, yellow belt. His hair and beard were copper colored and gleamed in the sun.

"Nothing good, friend Akohath," Caleb boomed, not seeming to care who was listening. "There are always those who think they know better than Moses and Aaron and imagine that they know better than God himself."

Akohath grasped Caleb's hand and wrist in greeting. "You know," Akohath said, "that my right arm is with the cause of Moses and Aaron, for I know that their word is from the Lord."

"I know it, Akohath," said Caleb, slapping a friendly hand on his shoulder, "but there are those who doubt your loyalty because your father likes the ways we left behind in Egypt too much."

"My father is my father," said Akohath warmly. "My life is his. But let no one doubt that I am the Lord's man and that I keep his Law."

"His law," came a rough, sneering voice. "Moses' law, you mean, and Aaron's law. What kind of law puts meat on one man's table and curds and mush on his brother's?"

Kevin glanced up sharply to see who it was with sentiments so much like Lamech's.

He saw a short, heavyset man with a grizzled beard, thick lips, and flaring nostrils. Over his colored tunic he wore an orange, wool cloak. His hair and skin glistened and he reeked of a long accumulation of sweat.

"Aaron is not taking meat off any man's table, Dathan," Caleb retorted. "When an animal is sacrificed, Aaron gets a portion. What's so bad about that? Is there not always a loaf for the baker, a skin for the tanner and some goat's hair for the tentmaker? Are we in Egypt where men pay for their needs with rings of silver?"

"Pah!" spat Dathan, and Kevin jumped out of his way. "No one has asked Aaron to be our butcher. My servants have knives. I can sacrifice an animal as well as Aaron can."

Caleb stared at Dathan until the latter looked away. "You know why all animals must be brought to Aaron or his family to be slaughtered," Caleb said.

"Pah!" Dathan spat again and moved off angrily, accompanied by a rough-looking detachment of his own household.

"What do you suppose all that was about?" said Kevin.

"Beats me," said Moshe. He looked about uneasily. Up until now he and Kevin had had very little contact with the people into whose time they had stumbled. Eber and Lamech were rough and nasty, but they were tanners. Korah had had them flogged, but even he had been courteous enough until he saw the hog on Kevin's T-shirt. And Akohath and his family—they were kind and caring people. Last night, when Akohath had been so troubled over the conflict between his duty to his father and his duty to his neighbor, Moshe had wanted to tell him the good news about Jesus. Wouldn't Akohath be surprised to learn that the God he worshiped would come to Earth as a man!

But these men in the crowd—Dathan and his crew, and most of the others—how could these be the children of Israel from whom Jesus came? Everywhere Moshe looked, knots of poor, dirty, angry men stood in rumpled garments, shaking their fists.

"Let's walk around and see if we can see anything besides backs," said Kevin. "Akobath is going to be occupied for a while, I think."

"OK," said Moshe. "If this is the town square, you'd think the Tabernacle and the altar ought to be around here someplace." The boys turned to see if anyone was watching them. Akohath was in earnest conversation with Caleb and some others who had joined them. To help them find their way back, they noted that Akohath was in front of a blue curtain that had some red tassels dangling at the entrance. Then they shouldered their way through the noisy, gesticulating crowd of men.

"Kind of reminds me of an archaeologists' convention," Moshe observed, "everybody standing around between sessions waving their arms and arguing their favorite theories."

"Except for the smell," said Kevin. "Look at that blackened altar. What a stench! I'm beginning to think that old Korah has the right idea about burning lots of incense. I'm for anything that would cover up all these awful smells. Hey! What's that over there?"

Moshe looked where Kevin was pointing. He could make out an open space beyond the altar, past the edge of the crowd.

"Something important. Looks like a sentry on duty, two of them," said Moshe. "In front of a blue tent. Look at the silver and gold tent posts!"

Eagerly the boys pressed on past the edge of the crowd toward the intriguing tent. It was nothing like the rough skin and goat's hair tents they had seen up to now. It was smaller than the others and made of some kind of rich woven blue, purple, and red cloth. An awning of the same cloth, supported by polished wooden posts, shaded the entrance.

The sentries stood like two statues, iron-pointed spears in their right hands, their left hands resting on the handles of bronze swords thrust into wide blue belts.

"The Tabernacle!" breathed Moshe. "Kevin, we're already in the Tabernacle. This tent must house the Holy Place and the Holy of Holies that only Aaron can enter. The ark is in there, the Ark of the Covenant! And the Ten Commandments, too!"

Moshe glanced at Kevin to see if his unbelieving friend was feeling any of the awe and excitement that he was. But Kevin was not looking at either the sentries or the doorway. He was gazing at some object near the canopy. The look on his face was not awe but utter amazement.

Moshe looked up. There, fixed firmly on a frame beside the entrance to the tent, was a silver candlestick, gleaming blindingly in the morning sun. It was their candlestick—the menorah from the Exodus dig that had brought them there. No black on it now, and no point at the foot, its base was flat where it was fastened to a frame.

"This has got to be it," Kevin said hoarsely. "It's standing on a frame. That is our doorway back into our own time, I'm sure of it. We've got to go through that doorway!"

"Are you crazy?" Moshe gasped. "That's too close to the doorway into the Holy Place. They'll kill us before they'll let us get anywhere near the tent."

Kevin broke into a run for the frame.

# 10
# Sacrifice of Blood

The two sentries sprang into action. Moving quickly, as if they were one man, they poised their spears to strike down anyone who would come near the beautiful tent.

"No, Kevin. No!" Moshe dragged at his friend, but desperation made the other boy stronger and Moshe was pulled after him towards the dully gleaming points of the lowered spears.

Moshe hung on to Kevin and suddenly stronger arms than his were yanking them back.

"I told you to stand close to me!" Akohath barked. "They would have killed you. That is the Holy Place of God! Of all the people of Israel only Moses and Aaron may enter there."

Kevin tried to tell Akohath about the candlestick on the frame next to the entrance to the Holy Place, but his words were drowned by a strange wailing, as of some huge animal in pain.

"The ram's horn," Akohath shouted. "Moses and Aaron are coming out. Over here. We can see and hear well from the side."

With Kevin restrained between them, Moshe and Akohath hurried to a place where they could see. Two men held their hands up to quiet the crowd. Both of them were old and wore their white beards long. One was broad shouldered and thick necked and wore something that looked like a flowing toga of blue, purple, and red cloth embedded with jewels.

The other was tall and, although obviously very old, stood erect. His simple white tunic was belted by a wide band of blue cloth and he held a rough staff in his right hand.

Moshe had no doubt that he was looking at his venerable namesake.

The man with the jeweled tunic, obviously Aaron, stepped through the crowd and stood by the altar that the boys had seen directly in front of the Holy Place.

Aaron spoke in a loud voice that carried over the crowd. He spoke in short, deliberate phrases, pausing after each. In the pauses, other voices, farther back in the crowd, repeated his words for the benefit of the people too far away to hear Aaron himself. The effect was rather like the echo of a loudspeaker at a football game.

Moshe became aware of a heavy, unpleasant odor that was wafted towards them on an occasional puff of wind from the direction of Aaron and the altar.

"Let any who have beasts ... to be sacrificed ... come forward," shouted Aaron. "When this is done ... the Lord Moses ... will speak."

A man with a scrawny goat pushed forward.

"A ram of the flock of Abiram, Lord," the man said sullenly, proffering the goat. Kevin and Moshe could see the animal's ribs from their vantage point.

"Is this the offering you make to the Most High God?" thundered Aaron. "Begone, both you and your goat. The Lord God will not be mocked. Let a perfect animal—the choicest of the herd—be brought as a sacrifice to God."

The man ran out of the square, dragging his bleating goat behind him.

Another man stepped forward. "I have sinned against God. May the Lord God accept this sacrifice and spare my life." He stooped to pick up a beautiful white sheep—whiter than any sheep Kevin or Moshe had ever seen.

"The Lord God will accept your gift and will let you live," said Aaron. "Place your hands on the sheep's head, for it will become your substitute."

The man did as he was told, then took up a knife and slit its throat. Two broad-shouldered men, younger versions of Aaron, came forward with their knives. With quick, practiced motions they upended the sheep and let the blood from its throat drain into a bowl. Aaron took the bowl and sprinkled the blood over the altar.

With swift slashes of the knife, one of the young men skinned the beast and then, with the easy skill of a butcher behind the glass of a supermarket, the other proceeded to cut the carcass into quarters. He laid the pieces on the altar, along with the head and entrails. Two other men lit the firewood under the altar and soon the flames leaped up to consume the sacrifice.

The scene was reenacted several times as men brought up two more goats, three young rams, and a pair of turtledoves. Sometimes certain pieces of meat would be given to Aaron instead of being burned.

As the sun grew hotter, the smell grew stronger. Moshe realized that the heavy odor that clung to the place was that of the blood of previous slaughters. But there was still another smell, a strong, yet strangely sweet odor. And it was not coming from the altar. Moshe glanced around, sniffing as deeply as he could, to detect the origin of the fragrance. Then he saw it. Behind and above Aaron, rising languidly to the sky, was a thin, black column of smoke. Moshe's eye followed the smoke down to its origin. It seemed to be coming from the tent of the Holy Place. Moshe looked at Kevin, who was gazing at the smoke, too.

"Moshe, look! That must be incense," said Kevin, pointing upward as discreetly as possible.

Their concentration was broken by the blow of a horn. Moses was holding up his arms to get the crowd's attention.

# 11
# Murmurs of Mutiny

"Hear, O Israel, the Lord Thy God is One!" the voice that rang out across the multitude of Israelites was as firm and strong and resonant as a temple gong.

The words came back from a thousand lips. "Hear, O Israel, the Lord Thy God is One!"

Moshe felt a thrill travel from his head to his heels as his whole body vibrated with the voice of Israel, which for a fleeting moment was also one.

*Wow!* he thought, *What a power there is here when they are united!*

But the moment quickly passed and once more the multitude was a fragmented mob, frantic to state their grievances to their leader.

"You, Moses!" It was the voice of Dathan. "How long must we bring our beasts to be sacrificed by Aaron? How long will you and your brother take meat from our children's table?"

"You, Moses! I, Abiram, speak with Dathan. My servants know how to wield a knife as well as the sons of Aaron. We demand that you return to us what is our right. We will sacrifice our own beasts among our own tents. Are we not all the sons and daughters of Jacob, our forefather? Does the Most High God belong only to Moses and Aaron? And are we not free to serve our God?"

A sudden gust of wind whipped at Moses' beard. Standing tall and angry in the sunlight he looked like a painting Moshe had seen of him breaking the stone tablets.

"Free? Free? Yes, by the mighty hand of God you are free. But in your minds you are slaves still, slaves to the filthy practices of your former masters.

"You, Dathan! It was your right when we entered the wilderness to tend to the slaughter of your own beasts. But did you do right? No!" he thundered. "No! You poured out their blood as a libation to the demons of the earth! You made a sacrifice to a stone and metal god and kindled the wrath of the God who took you out of bondage. Sacrifice to false gods is an abomination to the Lord of Israel. He has made of us his special people. He has set us apart from the idol worshipers."

"Hear me, Moses!" shouted Abiram. "It is true, Dathan poured the libation, but I never did so. I did not sacrifice to other gods. I made my sacrifice to the one true God."

Moses turned his blazing eyes on Abiram. "And you had need to do so," he said with sarcasm. "How long do you think you can appease God with sacrifices, when in your heart you devise a new evil even at the altar? Tell me, how many cuts do you take from a living beast when you have no need for the whole animal?"

In a flash Moshe recalled the bleeding sheep that Lamech had mutilated. Perhaps this had been a common practice among others of the Israelites. Moshe felt like throwing up.

"A dumb beast," Abiram retorted. "What matter?"

"Did not the Lord God make the beasts as well as man?" shouted Moses. "Does not a beast bleed when it is cut? Though a sheep does not hurl curses on one that hurts it, nevertheless, it suffers in its flesh. The Lord God commands that you will not shed blood unnecessarily, for the blood is the life of his creatures."

A high, reedy voice rose above the murmuring that followed.

"Hear me! I am On, son of Peleth! What good is all this talk about slaughter and meat? How many of us do not have even a goat to milk, let alone animals to spare for slaughter? We are hungry, Moses. Where is the milk and honey you have promised? Our little ones are tired. Our stomachs groan for the fruit of the land, not this manna that is the same day after day. We would be better off in Egypt!"

Others took up the cry. "Egypt, Egypt, Egypt!"

"We had good food to eat in Egypt!"

"Would to God we had died in Egypt!"

A deep, determined voice battled to be heard over the uproar. "Hear me, hear Joshua, son of Nun. Listen, you complainers. Listen, you fainthearted cowards! I have seen the land of promise. Caleb has seen it. It is rich with crops and water. It is a place to feed your children until they burst. Stop your complaining. Follow us and God will give us this land now. Not next year. Not years from now. Now!"

"Lies!" came back the cry. "Lies! You and Caleb say it will be so easy, but the others who were with you say differently. They say there are giants in the land who will kill us and leave our bodies for the birds and the jackals. Give us a captain who will lead us back to Egypt. Better slaves with full bellies than free men starving in the wilderness!"

Caleb made himself heard. "Why do you believe cowards? The land is an exceedingly good land. Trust in the Lord and don't fear the people who are there. With the Lord on our side, they don't have a chance against us. Only trust ..."

Caleb's words were cut off by a rock that struck him squarely in the chest. Another rock hit him on the right shoulder and as he put up his arms to protect his head, another caught him on the elbow. Now rocks were whizzing on every side. Moshe saw Aaron push Moses back to the safety of the tent. Men with javelins moved among the crowd, knocking rocks out of hands and ordering the people to disperse. Akohath grabbed Moshe and Kevin roughly by the arms and propelled them back the way they had come.

"There will be no chance to talk to Moses or any of the elders today," he said as they fought their way through the milling mass of bodies. "It is well that the Sabbath begins at sundown. It will give tempers a chance to cool."

The main crowd dispersed fairly quickly, but as Akohath and the boys made their way back to Korah's compound, they were aware of small angry groups talking earnestly and looking over their shoulders as if they would not be overheard.

"Look, there's Lamech," Kevin said.

Lamech was with a group that surrounded Dathan and seemed to be receiving instructions. Dathan spoke and Lamech nodded several times.

"Isn't that the guy whose kid had so much fun pulling the legs off that beetle?" said Kevin.

"Yes," said Moshe. "His name is Abiram, and there's the one that was with him. Looks like they're planning something."

"I wouldn't put it past that bunch to have started the rock throwing."

"You'd be wise to bridle your tongues," Akohath said shortly. "When rocks and words begin to fly, either can mean death to the unwary."

At Akohath's tent the slave Guerin was eagerly listening to the account of the riot from another slave who had been there.

"Guerin," Akohath called, "these are my guests. Show them how to purify themselves for the Sabbath."

Sullenly Guerin left his companion to stand by Moshe and Kevin.

"Treat them with courtesy," Akohath warned.

"Yes, Lord," muttered Guerin. He motioned for Moshe and Kevin to follow him. When they were safely out of Akohath's hearing, he began to grumble. "Slaves one day, guests the next!" he muttered. "How is anybody supposed to know how to act around some people if they're slaves one day, guests the next!"

"Sorry, Guerin," laughed Kevin. "Maybe you ought to start treating everybody the same whether they're slaves or not."

"Sure, Guerin," said Moshe. "You know what the Scriptures say, 'God is no respecter of persons.'"

Guerin looked at Moshe suspiciously. "What's that supposed to mean?" he demanded.

"It means that as far as God is concerned, a slave is just as good as a free man, and a stranger is just as good as a Hebrew."

Guerin's mouth dropped open in astonishment. "Is that what Moses says?"

"Sure is," said Moshe. "It also means that even if a man is free and very rich, he can't get away scot-free when he does something bad."

"Hmph!" grunted Guerin. "No wonder most of the lords won't let their slaves go to the meetings."

Guerin went on ahead, shaking his head in

amazement.

"I'll say one thing for Moses," said Kevin. "He's got his work cut out for him."

# 12

# Sabbath Breaker

The purification ritual consisted of taking a bath in a shallow stream behind the camp.

The gritty water made their lash marks sting, but it was the closest thing to a bath the boys had had since arriving in the time of Moses, and they felt refreshed by it.

"How many days have we been here?" Moshe asked. "It seems like we've been here forever, but this is the first Sabbath."

"Maybe Eber and Lamech don't observe the Sabbath," said Kevin.

Moshe shrugged. "Maybe not," he said. "But I kind of think that Eber would, even if Lamech didn't. I guess we could have arrived during a Saturday night and the sentry found us on Sunday morning. Sure has been a long week."

At Akohath's tent Miriam put some more salve on their wounds, and the family sat down to the evening meal. Akohath asked the Sabbath blessing and his wife gave each a tiny portion of wine.

"Until we get into the land of promise," she explained, "wine can only be a Sabbath luxury. Wanderers do not grow many grapes and poor people cannot trade for what they wish."

Kevin frowned. "Excuse me," he said politely, "but I have heard that your people took large flocks and much gold and silver jewelry from Egypt when you left to find the promised land."

Akohath laughed. "Then you must not have heard that we were slaves in the land of Egypt. Where would we get so much treasure? To be sure, some of us were better off than others. My own father was a slave in an Egyptian temple where he often received gifts of food, fine clothing, and gold."

"Abiram and Dathan," said Tamar, "had masters who rewarded their work with a yearly gift of lambs and kids for their own use. They had quite a flock of their own when we left."

Miriam sniffed. "I think they came out of Egypt with some of their master's animals that were never given to them."

"That may be, Daughter," said Akohath severely, "but the Lord commands us to speak no evil of our neighbor unless we have proof."

"I was told," Kevin persisted, "that before Moses led you out, he told all the women to go to their Egyptian neighbors and borrow all the valuable jewelry they could. Then, when you left, you took it all with you."

Akohath's wife's mouth fell open in astonishment. "Why, what utter nonsense!" she exclaimed. "Why, that would have been stealing! Why, what a thing to say! My mother would have stayed there and let Moses go on without her before she would have done such a thing!"

"Maybe I got the story wrong," Kevin offered.

Akohath nodded. "True," he said, "some details

often change when a story goes around."

Miriam looked searchingly at her mother. "What about that gold bracelet with the little blue stone in it, Mother?" she asked. "Is that not Egyptian work? And I remember a box full of shiny jewelry when I was a child."

"And what of it?" exclaimed Tamar. "What are you saying, Miriam?"

"I'm not saying anything, Mother," Miriam said quickly. "I'm just asking you where you got it, that's all. If that jewelry is really gold, then it seems it would be very valuable, wouldn't it?"

Tamar looked from Moshe to Kevin in some embarrassment. "It was a gift," she said.

Akohath laughed. "Maybe there is some truth to the rumor after all," he teased.

Tamar tossed her head angrily. "I did not steal it!" she exclaimed. "Not all the Egyptians were heartless brutes. The woman my mother worked for was as much her friend as her mistress. Her name was, oh, I don't remember the Egyptian word, but in our language her name meant Lotus Flower. I remember her as a very tall, beautiful lady with elaborate black makeup all round her eyes. After the last plague, Lotus Flower seemed to know that we weren't coming back. Maybe her husband had told her of Pharaoh's decree to throw us out of the country. Anyway, the night before we left she came to my mother and gave her a box of gold jewelry and that turquoise bracelet so that Mother could purchase food on our travels. Mother had asked her for a little help, but she never expected so much generosity. Many people have told me that the same thing happened to them."

A brief silence fell upon them. Then Akohath spoke, his dark eyes bright with emotion. "It has always been a matter of great wonder to me," he

said, "how we can love our enemies and they us."
The words were spoken with a finality that signaled
the end of the meal. Supper over, Akohath and his
family prepared for bed.

Moshe and Kevin were again given a place to
sleep inside the tent. There would be no work tomorrow on the Sabbath.

The next morning, Kevin and Moshe found themselves awake early even though they had permis-
sion to sleep in. Miriam was brimming with energy
and humor. "Up, up, you slugabeds," she cried,
when she saw them moving. "We're going to pack
up our Sabbath food and have our midday meal in
the forest!"

"The forest?" exclaimed Kevin. "What forest?"

"Well, it's not much of a forest," Miriam admitted,
"just a few old trees and a lot of dead branches on
the ground. It might have been a forest once,
though, so I call it one."

"And so you might say our little stream might have
been a river once," said her father, "and shall we
then call it the Nile?"

Miriam laughed and went on with her preparations.

"Are you permitted to carry things on the Sabbath?" Moshe asked as he watched her lay out five
portions of food.

"As long as everyone carries his own portion," she
said, "it is permitted. And if I choose to wrap my
portion in a cloth big enough for all of us to sit on,
who is to mind?"

Each member of the family, and Moshe and
Kevin, collected his portion and together the picnic
party set out for Miriam's "forest."

Mutiny, rock hurling, and barbaric practices
seemed far away as the happy group made its way
past the encampment to the open country. Kevin, or

"Kevi" as Miriam preferred to call him, had a hilarious time teaching her how to whistle.

Suddenly a shout drew their attention. "Hello there! Lord Akohath! I would speak to you!" It was Eber, waving and keeping his distance.

"Friend Eber!" Akohath called back. "What news?"

"I need to send a message to the elders. Since you have taken away my two slaves there, and Lamech is gone most of the time, my work goes very slowly. Please to ask them if they can find me some help."

"How is it that Lamech is gone?" asked Akohath.

"That I don't know. I believe he is spending most of his time with Dathan and as he is free and no slave, it is his right. He could have told me, though, and not just gone off as he has. The lads I can understand. Who would be a tanner's slave if he could help it? But Lamech, now, I thought the choice was his. No matter, though, he's gone and my back is not what it used to be and no son to pass the trade on to, so if the elders want to keep the tanyard running, they'd best look to it. Good Shabbosh to you, and to you, too, lads. Old Eber wishes you well, be sure of that."

"Thank you, Eber," Moshe called, "and we you."

"Speak for yourself," Kevin muttered, "seeing him just brings back all the sweat and smell of that horrible place and the humiliation of being slaves."

When Miriam tried to reopen the whistling lesson, Kevin ignored her and stalked along silently. Moshe fell into step with him. "Snap out of it, Kevin," he said. "Akohath and his family are being really decent."

"Sure they are," Kevin said bitterly, "and what happens if he takes us before the elders tomorrow and the elders decide that we should be slaves? Then what? Back to the tanyard for the rest of our lives?"

Kevin's dark mood was no match for Miriam, however. She soon had him back in the spirit of her outing.

"Let's spread the cloth here, Kevin," she directed. "That way we can't see the camp and can see those three trees in a row and can pretend we're deep in a cool cedar forest in the land of promise."

"My daughter, the dreamer!" said Tamar.

"Let us thank God for the dreamers," said Akohath. "It is they who lead the doers."

The sun sank slowly as the picnickers enjoyed their meal, talking or remaining silent as the mood took them. A sense of peace and contentment had cast its spell on all of them and Moshe and Kevin felt as if they were as much a part of the family as Miriam.

"Poor Eber!" Miriam exclaimed, when no one had spoken for a long time.

"What 'poor Eber'?" asked Tamar. "Who said anything about Eber?"

"I was just thinking how nice it is sitting here, all of us together," said Miriam, "enjoying each other's company and the Sabbath and being part of a family, and then I thought of how Eber gave up his family and sent his wife and son to live with another man and never sees them except at a distance ..."

"OK, OK," exploded Kevin. "We get the idea!"

Tamar sighed. "Poor Eber," she agreed. "Better he had never married. Not one woman in a thousand could bear to be a tanner's wife."

Miriam snorted. "She'd be better off if she'd stayed with the tanner."

"Why?" asked Moshe. "What happened to her?"

"She's married to Abiram," said Miriam. "And a meaner, crueler man there isn't in all Israel."

"Miriam!" Akohath admonished her. "Speak no evil."

"Well, he is, Father," she insisted. "And he's turned

that darling little boy into a monster. I saw him the other day sitting on a donkey beating it over the ears with a tent peg and there stood Abiram, laughing as if it was the cutest thing in the world. And when he was still with Eber, even as young as he was, he wouldn't have hurt a fly."

A memory began to trouble Moshe. "How old would Eber's son be now?"

"About four," said Miriam.

"Would his name happen to be Seth?" he asked.

"Why, yes!" said Miriam, "how did you know? They say that Eber has never spoken his name since he had to give him up."

"I've met him," said Moshe. He was silent for a time, recalling the child squatting in the dirt, methodically pulling the legs off the beetle. "Poor Eber," he said at last.

The gaiety and contentment had gone out of the picnic.

Akohath stood up and stretched. "I'm ready to be getting back," he said. "Tomorrow we will try to get to the tent of meeting earlier to get the attention of one of the elders."

As Kevin helped Miriam fold the cloth, Akohath gazed about. "Look at that!" he exclaimed.

The others followed his gaze. "What's so great about that?" Kevin asked carelessly. "Some guy picking up sticks and putting them in a sack. So what?"

"It's the Sabbath," Miriam said in a subdued voice. "He's gathering sticks on the Sabbath!"

"Uh, oh," said Kevin. "That has a familiar ring to it. Didn't something bad happen to somebody who was gathering sticks on the Sabbath?"

"Uh-huh," said Moshe. "And can you see who it is?"

Kevin shaded his eyes against the lowering sun.

"Who?"

"It's Lamech," said Moshe. "And he seems to be whistling."

# 13

# "Stone Him! Stone Him!"

It was amazing how quickly a pointing, murmuring crowd gathered to gape at the figure of Lamech gathering sticks under the Sabbath sun.

The murmur swelled to a roar and then the shout went up.

"Sabbath breaker!"

"Sabbath breaker!"

"Stone him!"

"Stone him!"

A few stones had been thrown when the armed guards that served Moses appeared in a rush and surrounded the offender.

"Would you stone a man on the Sabbath?" shouted the leader. "We will take this man to Moses. Tomorrow, at the tent of meeting, it will be decided what to do. Go to your tents. The Sabbath breaker is in our hands."

Grumbling, the crowd parted to let the armed men pass with their prisoner.

"What do you think will be done with him?" Moshe asked Akohath.

Korah's son shook his head. "It will be bad, I fear," he said. "But it is idle for me to speculate. It is Moses who will decide." The picnic thus interrupted, the family headed back to their tents to spend the rest of the Sabbath in leisure.

On the following day, when Moses came out of his tent to hear the case against Lamech, Akohath and the boys were on the front row .

"Is it true what these witnesses say," Moses asked, "that you were gathering sticks on the Sabbath?"

Lamach stood defiantly before the white-haired leader. "You have said," he growled insolently.

"Do you not know that the Lord God has given us the Sabbath as a sign that we are his people? We are forbidden to work on the Sabbath for it is holy. It is a day to rest and renew our spirits and to think of our God and give him thanks for all his gifts. Did you know this when you gathered sticks? I ask again because there is one punishment for the man who breaks the Law in ignorance and another for him who does so in knowledge of what he does."

"He knows!" one of the witnesses spoke up. "Not four Sabbaths since he was doing the same thing. He did it in defiance of the Law, in defiance of the Almighty God who gave us the Law."

"I saw him, too. Let's stone him!" someone in the crowd shouted.

"Silence!" roared Moses. "You, Lamech, there are two witnesses against you," he said. "Why did you gather the sticks?"

"I needed some firewood," Lamech said.

"Why could you not wait to gather your firewood until after Sabbath was over?"

"I was hungry and I wanted to cook my supper."

A gasp went up from the crowd, but Moshe thought he also heard some of the men laugh.

Moses glanced shrewdly over the crowd. "There will be no fire kindled on the Sabbath, for it is holy," he said. "All food for the Sabbath must be cooked the day before. Did you not know this?"

"I know that I was hungry," said Lamech. "When I'm hungry, I eat."

"Why do you stand there listening to this man's insolence, Moses?" one of the witnesses demanded. "It is clear that he broke the Sabbath in knowledge and in defiance of the Law. The punishment is clear. Why do you wait?".

Moshe was close enough to see the emotions that played over the face of Moses. There was strength and purpose in those features, but there, too, he saw pain and hesitation.

"What's the trouble, Moses?" came a mocking voice that might have belonged to Dathan. "Can't you make up your mind what to do? Maybe it's time we had a new leader, one that knows his mind."

An ugly murmuring surged through the crowd. It was clear to Moshe that this was not merely a question of one man's breach of the Sabbath. It was a test, a carefully set up challenge to the authority of Moses and his conviction about the importance of the Law.

"Silence!" shouted Aaron, who stood beside his brother. "Silence! Moses speaks."

Aaron turned and looked hard at his brother. Moses breathed deeply and spoke. "It is a heavy thing to take a man's life," he said. "But it is better that one man die than the whole people be cut off. God has given us the Sabbath and commanded us to keep it holy. In willfully breaking the Sabbath, Lamech has trangressed the Law and brought sin on all the people. Lamech, you must die. The witnesses must cast the first stones."

At these words, ready hands reached out and pulled Lamech into the seething mass of people. Pushed, yanked and prodded, he was borne out of the meeting square to the outskirts of the encampment, and Moshe and Kevin found themselves moving helplessly with the rest.

"Stone him! Stone him! Stone him!" The shout took on the rhythms of a chant.

In an open space strewn with rocks, Lamech, already bruised and bleeding from many small cuts on his face and arms, was thrown down and the crowd ringed itself round him. Moshe noticed that women and children joined the men and started snatching up rocks.

Lamech shielded his head with his arms as the first barrage of rocks flew about him. Moshe recalled his dream in which the tall, golden champion stood between him and the mob and took the missles on his own flesh.

Lamech had no such champion. Soon the thick, muscular body sagged under the rain of rocks and he sank groaning to the ground, unable to rise. Some of the stoners on the front ranks went close and prodded the motionless body with their feet, shrugged and turned away. Two men dragged the body and hung it in a tree. It was over. Their anger spent, the people made their way silently back to the encampment. Only Moshe and Kevin remained, watching the motionless form hanging suspended from the branches.

"I'm going to go over and see if ... if ... you know." said Moshe weakly.

Kevin could not speak.

Moshe stood beside Lamech. He thought he saw a flicker under the blood of his eyelids.

"Lamech?"

The eyes opened and Lamech looked out.

"I'm, I'm sorry, Lamech," was all that Moshe could think to say. He wished he had some water or a wet cloth or something to ease the man's final moments.

"I pray that God will have mercy on your soul," Moshe said.

Lamech's lips moved. With a great effort he spoke. "I ... spit ... on ... you ... all," he said, and he died.

"Let's go," Kevin said hoarsely.

The glistening flies were beginning to settle on Lamech's face.

"We can't just leave him like this overnight or the dogs will eat him," Moshe said.

"Why not?" said Kevin. "What was he to us? A brute and an animal. Leave him."

"You go," said Moshe. "I'm going to cover him up."

Moshe pulled Lamech's body off the tree and began to cover it with the rocks that lay scattered around him. Slowly and methodically, he picked them up and put them down as Kevin stood several paces away, his hands dangling by his sides.

"You're being stupid," Kevin said.

"Maybe," grunted Moshe, stooping, lifting and putting down. "I just know that I wouldn't want to be left that way."

"Stupid," Kevin repeated, but he bent to the task with Moshe and together they built a tomb for Lamech.

# 14
# Cracks in the Earth

The encampment was buzzing with talk of open rebellion when they got back.

Akohath told them that even as Lamech was being stoned, Dathan and Abiram were stirring up the people of their own tribe against Moses for pronouncing the death penalty for something like collecting firewood on the Sabbath.

"They have put a line of armed men around their part of the camp, and they have defied Moses or his agents to enter. They say that they will no longer bring their animals to Aaron to be sacrificed."

As the afternoon wore on, the women went about their usual tasks, but the men stood about talking in low voices. There was an unusual amount of traffic going toward the section of the camp inhabited by Dathan and his people. Eyes and looks were furtive.

"I get the feeling," said Kevin, "that an awful lot of these people who haven't already sifted into Dathan's tents are ready to do it if Moses shows the least sign of weakness."

"Are you forgetting something, Kevin?" Moshe asked.

"What?" said Kevin.

"These people are just waiting to see what happens. We know what's going to happen."

Kevin was genuinely puzzled. "I don't know what you're talking about."

"Numbers," said Moshe. "You've read it as well as I have. It's in the Book of Numbers. Don't you remember the rebellion of Dathan and Abiram? It's all mixed in with something to do with the tribe of Levi and how they were jealous of Aaron and his sons."

"I know the part you mean," said Kevin. "Three or four guys lead the rebellion. I never paid much attention to their names. Some are destroyed by fire from heaven, and others are swallowed up by an earthquake."

Kevin looked at Moshe for a long time and then laughed harshly. "You've got to be kidding, Moshe! I know you believe in a lot of religious stuff, but an earthquake! In this part of the country? The geology's all wrong even if you wanted to argue a coincidence. No way."

Moshe shrugged and went to look for Tamar to see if she had anything she wanted done. She put him to work braiding flax into rope. He was glad to have something to do. The sense of waiting was growing heavy, like an invisible weight over the whole camp.

When the sun was about midway in its afternoon course, the eerie wail of the ram's horn floated over the encampment. Everywhere people stopped what they were doing and lifted their heads in alarm. It was the sound of authority. Moses was ready to act.

As the wail died away, all that could be heard in the camp was the sound of men's sandaled feet hitting the dry earth. Moshe left his work and followed the sound. Kevin caught up with him, and they saw the armed agents of Moses tramping between the rows of tents toward the defended compound of Dathan and Abiram.

The boys followed with a great many others and stopped when the soldiers stopped, facing the tents of Dathan.

Behind the line of armed men, the life of the compound was going on much as usual. Women squatted at their grindstones or worked at their looms while children tumbled at their feet. Here and there men too old to stand with the sentries sat and stared.

"Dathan and Abiram, come out!"

The speaker was a tall, thick-necked man with a deep voice and a scar that ran from his left nostril to his jaw. "Hear the words of your leader Moses!" he shouted.

The flap of a large tent pushed open and Dathan shouldered his way out followed by Abiram and the hungry-looking man who had identified himself at the meeting as On, son of Peleth.

Dathan put his hands on his hips and spat in the direction of the soldiers. "Who is Moses?" he shouted back. "I am leader here. My men also are armed. We are no friendless Lamechs, naked and unarmed. Go back if you value your skin and tell your Moses that he is not leader here."

The messenger stood his ground. "The Lord Moses commands that you appear before him at the tent of meeting for his judgment. You are to come at once, On, son of Peleth, Dathan and Abiram, sons of Eliab, and all your chief men. It is the command of Moses, servant of the Mighty God."

Dathan shook his fist at the messenger. "Tell him that we will not come! Tell him that we are *all* God's

105

people, not just Aaron and Moses."

On, son of Peleth, waved his skinny arms excitedly. "Who is he to make himself and his brother princes over us?" If he wants to talk to us, he can come here!"

Dathan, Abiram, and On contemptuously turned their backs on the delegation and went back into the tent. Ignoring the jeers of the people in Dathan's compound, the messenger signaled his men and they went back the way they had come.

"I don't see what Moses can possibly do now," said Kevin, "to save face, I mean. It was one thing to set the mob to stone Lamech. He was a kind of outcast to begin with. But Dathan is powerful. He practically has his own army."

"You're forgetting what Moses has that Dathan hasn't," said Moshe.

"Sure," Kevin said sarcastically, "lightning bolts and earthquakes."

The boys continued to loiter with the other spectators in front of the tents of Dathan. The sense of waiting grew heavier. Not many people spoke and when they did they kept their voices hushed.

The abnormal quiet was pierced by the uncanny tone of the ram's horn. Again came the sound of feet hitting the hard ground. The soldiers were returning and this time Moses and Aaron walked in front.

"I never thought he'd come himself!" exclaimed Kevin.

"Why not?" asked Moshe.

"Face," said Kevin. "He lost face before when Dathan treated his messenger with contempt, but this time there's no way he can come out leader. Unless his army can whip Dathan's and it looks to me as if Dathan has him outnumbered and outarmed.

"Now that he's here in person, all the humiliation

will fall on him directly. If he tells Dathan to shape up and Dathan spits in his eye, all Moses can do is turn around and go back to his tent."

Moses took up his position across from Dathan's tent.

There was a flurry about the tent as On hurried out and disappeared around the side at an awkward running walk.

Neither Dathan nor Abiram came out, although they had to know that Moses was there. Aaron leaned towards his brother and said something to him. Moses shook his head.

On, son of Peleth, reappeared followed by a slave who was pulling a reluctant goat along by the horns. The flap of the tent moved and a dark-haired child tumbled out. It was Seth, the tanner's child, who now belonged to Abiram. He immediately clambered onto the back of the goat and jumped up and down, kicking its sides with his heels. A woman, Moshe supposed it was the boy's mother, Eber's former wife, pulled him off. Seth resisted furiously, pummeling and kicking her as mercilessly as he had the goat. She dropped him in front of the tent and got out of his way. She went back in and came out with a brazier filled with lighted coals. On, son of Peleth, brought a tripod and Seth's mother set the brazier on it.

"Still no sign of Dathan," commented Kevin. "He's going to make Moses call him. He knows how to play it for all it's worth."

Several minutes more passed and still Dathan did not condescend to come out of the tent. At last he got what he wanted. Moses called to him. "Dathan, come out! I speak for the Lord of Israel."

The tent flap moved and Dathan came out, followed by Abiram. "Indeed, Moses," Dathan shouted back, "I, too, speak for the Lord of Israel. You yourself have told us that God is the God of the whole congregation and that we are all of us holy to the Lord. How is it then that you and Aaron lift yourselves up above the congregation to say what the master of a household can or cannot do?"

"I have never denied the rights of a man to be master of his own household," replied Moses. "I do not ask you to obey my wishes. I am only a servant myself, the keeper of God's holy Law. It is his Law that you wish to break. It is God, not I, whom you must obey."

Dathan laughed harshly for the benefit of his listeners. "Then it is he, not you, who must make me obey!" he retorted. "I say that it is no offense to God for a man to sacrifice his own beasts to God. I say also if our fathers made offerings, it is no offense for *us* to make offerings. Behold, old man, what I, Dathan, will do!"

Dathan made a rapid series of commands and gestures and his people sprang to obey. One brought the goat, another a knife. Abiram's wife brought a large bowl and three burly slaves rolled a large rock over in front of his tent. Clearly Dathan planned to offer the ultimate defiance to the teachings of Moses. He was going to defy the prohibition. He was going to make a sacrifice right before Moses.

Moses lifted his hands in the gesture of prayer. "Respect not their offering, O Lord," he cried. "Remember your servant whom you have commanded, saying, to obey is better than sacrifice and to hearken than the fat of rams."

"I thought Samuel first said that," whispered Kevin.

"Maybe God said it to Moses, too," suggested Moshe.

Eyes blazing, Moses addressed the people. "Depart, depart, from the tents of these wicked men!

Flee from them, lest the wrath of God in destroying them destroy you also!"

Inside the compound there rose a burst of laughter from those nearest the leaders, but several of the people, including some of the sentries, scrambled to put some distance between themselves and the lawbreakers.

"Run, cowards!" shouted Dathan, "but do not think to return tomorrow."

"Hear me, Israel," shouted Moses, "if Dathan and his rebels see tomorrow, you shall know that the Lord has not sent me.

"But if the Lord does what no man expects, if the Lord makes the very earth to open up and swallow up these sinners and everything that belongs to them, and they go down alive into the pit, then you will know that these men have provoked the Lord!"

Like ants leaving a ruptured anthill, more of Dathan's people streamed out of his compound at the terrifying words of Moses, but the leaders and their families stood fast.

"Frighten slaves with your words, old man," shouted Dathan. "A free man does not tremble when an owl hoots. Give me the knife!"

Abiram put the knife into Dathan's hand as On, son of Peleth, pulled the goat's head back. Abiram's wife caught the blood in the basin as Dathan drew the knife across the animal's throat. Seth looked on with fascinated interest as Dathan made two quick cuts and pulled the goat's still beating heart from its body on the point of his knife. The heart he dropped onto the blazing coals in the brazier. Then he took the bowl and prepared to pour the blood ceremonially on the ground.

A low rumble as of thunder sounded ominously through the camp. Some more of Dathan's people deserted to the side where Moses stood. Slowly

Dathan knelt on one knee and poured the blood onto the ground. The rumble sounded again and the trickles of blood lengthened and deepened and became not trickles, but cracks.

Again the rumble sounded. It was not thunder but the earth, heaving and pitching. Dathan lurched and fell, facedown onto the blood offering as behind him all around rose terrified shrieks.

Dathan's tent swayed crazily and then, as the ground opened under it, sank in billowing folds of cloth and disappeared from sight. The brazier on which Dathan had offered the goat's heart toppled as the earth by it opened, and it, too, disappeared into the earth, scattering coals and licking flames.

The little boy, Seth, screaming frantically, ran towards his mother who held out her arms to him, but just as they reached each other the earth shifted again and they slid from sight in a tangle of arms and legs.

Behind him Moshe heard a hideous scream and was knocked to the ground as the frenzied form of Eber the tanner raced towards his wife and son. Before Eber could cross the line into Dathan's camp, the earth convulsed again creating a wide chasm and throwing Eber to the ground on the side where Moses stood.

Shifting and sliding sluggishly like cement in a mixer, the ground under Dathan's compound churned and swallowed the rebels, their families, their tents, their fires and ovens, the sacrificial altar, and everything that once belonged to Dathan who dared to defy the commandment of the Lord.

# 15
# Lord Korah's Test

A stunned silence hung over the encampment of the Hebrews for many days. No one met in the Tabernacle. The fires at the tannery went out as Eber, completely crazed, wandered about the earthquake site calling for his son.

Korah, too, seemed to have been touched in the mind by the awful demonstration of God's displeasure. But instead of turning away from his fascination with the trappings of Egyptian religion—the incense and the sun disk—he turned more openly towards them.

Leaving the work of his household in the hands of Akohath and his brother, Korah walked the camp from morning to night, dressed resplendently in his blue robes, the sun disk gleaming openly on his chest, stopping men, always with the same question. "Were you there?" he demanded. "Did you see the earth swallow Dathan?" And then, his voice subdued and plaintive and full of urging, he would say, "God is not pleased with our worship, you know. We

111

had all better work harder to gain God's favor."

Many of the men so accosted would shake themselves free and go their ways, tapping a finger to their foreheads. But some listened earnestly and day by day Korah attracted a following that met at his tent at sundown to be led in prayer at the setting of the sun.

Another Sabbath came and went without incident, but then, early on the day after the Sabbath, a week to the day since the stoning of Lamech and the destruction of the camp of Dathan, Korah led his fellow worshipers to the tent of meeting.

Akohath walked beside his father, pleading. "I beg you, Father," he said, "do not do this thing. Do not tempt the wrath of the most High God. Do not anger his servant Moses. You saw what happened to Dathan and Abiram and the rest. They defied the Law and they died and all their household with them."

"Dathan was an ignorant man," Korah said. "He did not know the right way to approach the most High God. I am no Dathan. I am learned in the ways of worship, and what I do, I do with respect and honor. You will see."

Korah led his following to the tent of Moses and asked for audience. Moses and Aaron came out to them.

Korah bowed courteously. "Hear our request, Moses," he said. "We believe that we need a priest in Israel, one learned in the ways of worship who will lead the people in the correct forms of prayer."

Aaron and Moses looked at Korah in utter disbelief. "Are you mad, Korah?" demanded Aaron. "Where is Dathan who seven days ago stood in this place defying my brother Moses? Get back to your tents while you yet live. Moses is your leader. God demands no superstitious acts, no worship of created things, and no more than his law requires."

"Moses is our teacher," Korah replied. "I honor Moses. Aaron is wise in council. I honor Aaron. But Aaron is no true priest, and Moses is no true priest. We cannot worship aright without a priest, who will give God even more dignity. It is not only I who think this."

"I agree with Korah!" shouted one of his followers.

"And I!"

"And I!"

It seemed to Moshe that about fifty men, there may have been more, rallied around Korah and shouted their agreement with him.

"In Egypt every Egyptian who led his household in prayer had his own censer and gold disk, was this not so?"

Moses was slow to answer. "This was so," he said finally. "But at Sinai we received a new covenant. The Lord of Israel does not require empty forms of worship. He requires worship of the heart. He requires obedience to his law and reverence, not incantations and child sacrifices and communication with dead things. He asks us to preform the prescribed sacrifices. He wants us to protect the widow and the orphan, to act justly towards our neighbors and the stranger in our midst. What you demand is vanity, Egyptian trumpery."

Korah set his jaw stubbornly. "Let us bring our censers before the Lord's Tabernacle," he said. "Let us worship him from our hearts with the ceremony our fathers learned in Egypt."

Moses glowered at Korah and his followers. "Is it not enough," Moses finally shouted, "that you are of the holy congregation? Must you attempt to change the covenant of God as he has shown it to me?"

"We do not seek to change anything," Korah

protested. "We seek only to honor the God who gave it to us. Let all who agree with me bring their censers before the Lord and worship him. If God, whose name no man may say, is pleased with me, let us then choose a priest who will lead the congregation in his worship as befits the most High God."

Shouts and cheers went up around Korah as he finished. Aaron and Moses conferred briefly, then Moses raised his hands for silence.

"Very well," he said. "It is a test. In the morning Aaron will meet you at the tent of meeting with his censer. You shall bring your own censer and shall select 250 people who are in agreement with you. They shall each bring their censers and stand with you before God. If you will have the Lord choose what is right and who is holy, so be it. But I say again, Korah, forget not Dathan."

Korah left the meeting in high spirits. "Moses will see," he said, "and so will Aaron. The most High God will have a true priest. And I will be that priest. I, Korah, will serve the Lord as priest in Israel."

Akohath kept a firm hold on his father's arm as they made their way home. The old man's voice was loud and confident and full of excitement. But his eyes held a strange glitter, like the eyes of a man with fever.

# 16
# Strange Fire

That night no one slept very much.

Korah was in and out of Akohath's tent with instructions and reminders which he delivered again and again.

"This lad will serve as my incense carrier," he said, pointing at Moshe for the fifth time, "and the other will be yours."

Ever since the earthquake it seemed that Korah had forgotten who Moshe and Kevin were. He no longer recognized them as "pig-worshiping slaves" but rather seemed to think that they belonged to Akohath's family.

"But, Father," Akohath protested each time, "I cannot carry a censer before the Tabernacle. I do not believe that that is the way God wishes us to worship him."

"Does not God teach you to honor your father?" Korah demanded severely.

"Yes, of course," Akohath replied, "and I do honor you, my father. But he also commands me to love him and have no other gods before him."

"Well, then," said Korah easily, "what's all the fuss about? No one is asking you to put other gods before him. All I'm asking you to do is take your censer and stand beside me and pray."

The exchange was repeated several times.

Moshe and Kevin retired to their sleeping places to avoid getting involved.

"You know what's coming, don't you?" Moshe whispered to Kevin, when Akohath again took his father home for the night.

"What?" said Kevin irritably, "more divine fun and games?"

"Look, Kevin," said Moshe, "you saw that earthquake as well as I did. You can't pretend that Dathan and the other rebels weren't swallowed up by the earth. It happened."

"Coincidence," said Kevin. "There was an earthquake and they were on it."

"I thought you said the geology was all wrong."

Kevin sulked for a while before he spoke. "So next it's fire from heaven, right?"

"That's what it says in the Bible. Earthquakes and fire from heaven. Korah and all his followers are next."

"Well, since we've been elected incense bearers, I guess that will take care of our little problem of being stuck in the past. We'll soon be unstuck."

"It's going to be dangerous, all right," said Moshe, "but I think this may be our chance to get home and I don't mean home to the Pearly Gates."

Kevin mover closer.

"What do you mean?"

"The Holy Place," said Moshe. "As leader Korah will probably stand nearest the tent of the Holy Place. In all the excitement we may have a chance to make a run for it and go through the doorway under the menorah."

Kevin sat up in his excitement.

"Yeah! And if I'm right, we'll be pulled back through the time vortex to our own time!"

The boys sat in silence for a few moments, savoring the thrill of renewed hope.

"And if I'm wrong?" Kevin said.

"Either way," said Moshe, "our troubles will be over."

Korah was in the tent before daylight, lighting lamps and shaking people awake.

"Up, up. Let's get things ready. You boys, here is the incense, the finest of Egyptian blends. I've been saving it for such an occasion."

Korah gave each boy an intricately carved box and carefully spooned incense into each from a larger container that he had.

"Take care not to spill it, lads," he said. "There's nothing like it outside the temple at Tanis."

Trusting little to his slaves, Korah was in and out, bringing the censer Akohath would use and various ornaments he had decided were essential to his son's dignity.

Akohath, worn down by his father's persistent appeal to his duty as a son, had at last agreed to be one of the censer bearers.

"Are you sure you want to do this, Husband?" Tamar asked, fear in her dark eyes.

"Sometimes one must do what one does not wish to do, my dear," he said. "I do not think that the God of Israel desires to be worshiped with incense. But I know that he wants me to honor my father."

Reluctantly Tamar helped Akohath into the splendid robes Korah had brought for him. She oiled his hair and beard and draped a gold chain around his neck.

117

"I will not wear the sun disk," he said firmly. "That I am convinced is idolatry."

He unfastened the gold symbol from the chain and gave it to Miriam who looked at it curiously and put it with her mother's combs and trinkets.

Requiring no elaborate preparations themselves, Moshe and Kevin went outside to wait. They took the boxes of the precious incense with them.

Kevin sniffed at his. "Yuck," he said. "Whoever got the idea this stuff smelled good?"

"I guess by contrast," suggested Moshe. "Sure smells better than a lot of the smells around here. I guess the earliest Egyptians started using it to cover up the ordinary day-to-day smells of cooking and sweating and stuff. Then they got the idea that their gods might like the smell, too, so they made it a part of their ritual. Sure beats the smell of dried blood."

They squatted in a sandy spot outside Akohath's tent. The sun was just beginning to light the encampment as the first of Korah's followers appeared carrying their censers.

"Say, Moshe," said Kevin thoughtfully, "what if, I say *If,* mind you, there is a God and he really doesn't want Korah and this lot to burn incense to him. Where does that leave Akohath?"

Moshe thought about it. "I guess since Akohath is just going along with it to show his respect for his father, he isn't really dishonoring God, he's just obeying God's command to honor his father."

"But on the other hand," said Kevin, "if Akohath burns incense in front of the Tabernacle along with all the others who stand against Moses and Aaron, he's breaking the Law. Regardless of *why* he's doing it, the fact remains that he *is* doing it."

"Even so," Moshe said, "Akohath isn't like the others. He accepts Moses as God's voice, and he tries to live the Law in everything he does. Surely God will make an exception in his case."

Kevin stared at the container of incense in his hand.

"I don't pretend to understand your view of the Christian God," he said. "I have never believed in God. But if that earthquake was no coincidence, then something is at work here, call it God. And if it is God, then one thing is very clear to me, he is consistent. I'd say that from his standpoint the Law is the Law and if Akohath goes through with this, he's going to be in big trouble."

The boys fell silent. Thoughtfully, Kevin traced patterns in the sand with his fingers. Around them Korah's supporters assembled with their censers and their incense bearers. The time grew near.

Moshe thought about Kevin's words. He did have a point. What was the story in the Bible about the man who tried to keep the Ark of the Covenant from falling off a cart? God had warned the people never to touch it. But this man saw the ark falling and had tried to save it. He had good intentions, but when he put up his hand to steady the ark, God struck him dead. Perhaps what a person did was more important than what he said. Moshe shuddered. This was an uncomfortable thought.

Moshe's contemplation was interrupted by the growing crowd of Korah's supporters, assembled with their censers and incense carriers. A shadow fell over Moshe. Someone had stepped in front of him.

"Are you ready, Drummond?" asked a voice. It was Akohath.

"Are you going to burn incense with your father?"

"I am not confident of my decision, Drummond. I do not feel that what my father is doing is right. The choice is not easy because my decision does not affect only myself. I represent my wife and daughter and ... you and Kevin, for you are guests in my

119

home."

Suddenly there was the blast of a ram's horn and Korah appeared in full regalia and assembled his group. He held up his arms and addressed the crowd. "We know what we do is right," shouted Korah. "Our God needs a noble priest—a priest who will initiate a fitting observance—the kind the Egyptians had. Whoever is for me, come forward. But whoever will follow Moses and Aaron, the self-made princes of the people, begone."

The crowd surged toward Korah and lined up before him. Moshe glanced at Akohath who stood motionless, gazing at his father.

"I will not join him," Moshe heard Akohath say under his breath. "I cannot be a part of this blasphemy."

Then aloud, "Kevin, you go to my home and tell my wife we will not be a part of my father's plan. Drummond, you come with me."

Moshe had difficulty keeping up with Akohath's long, quick strides. They pushed through the crowd and walked up to Korah, who was now seated on a throne carried by eight men.

"Where is your incense burner, my son?" demanded Korah, his eyes blazing. "Take your place of honor here beside the lord Korah. I shall make you the most important man of Israel—second only to me."

"No, my father," responded Akohath. "Please abandon your desire for this thing. God will be angry at your rebellion."

"Who are you to tell me what to do? Am I your donkey or your servant?" cried Korah. "No more foolishness. You shall be a part of this or I will have no part of you."

"Then you will have no part of me," said Akohath evenly. "Neither I, nor my house, nor any who dwell there will join in this blasphemy."

Moshe watched Korah's face. It turned red with rage and then changed abruptly. Korah laughed. Not a happy laugh, like the kind among friends, but a sinister one. Akohath waited for his father's reply.

"I will not be dishonored before Moses, Aaron, and these people by your disobedience. You shall join me. Guards! Seize this man."

Moshe saw the crowd part. Two men with drawn swords rushed at Akohath and grabbed him, wrestling with him until Akohath fell to the ground—two sword tips at his throat.

Moshe wanted to scream. He stood paralyzed for a moment, then he knew what he must do. He cautiously wriggled backward between the two men standing closest to him. He continued pushing his way through the crowd—hiding in the folds of one man's tunic, ducking past a man who was fanning the coals in his censer, slipping to the edge of the crowd. He had to save Kevin and Tamar and Miriam.

Moshe tried to look nonchalant as he walked toward the pathway that led to Akohath's tent. Once out of the crowd's line of vision, Moshe ran to the tent as fast as he could.

"Kevin, Miriam, Tamar, quick, come with me," Moshe said. "Lord Korah has arrested the lord Akohath. We are in danger. Let's escape and join sides with Aaron and Moses."

Tamar and Miriam looked at Moshe. "Tell us what has happened."

"No time. Come!" Moshe screamed. "We must go now." He grabbed their hands and had almost dragged them out of their tent before they could get to their feet.

The foursome ran as silently as they could, avoiding the populated areas of the camp. They slipped unseen past the outermost group of tents and crept through a pasture. Then they cut in sharply between two low tents and ran, stooping to avoid notice, toward the Tabernacle.

"There it is," said Kevin, pointing at the blue and purple and red panels of cloth that rose above the tops of the nearby tents.

"Miriam, Tamar," said Moshe, "hide yourselves by this tree. Kevin and I will try to get help inside."

But it was too late. Just as the boys pushed their way to the place where Moses and Aaron were standing, a ram's horn blew and all eyes focused on the grand procession entering the curtained square.

Korah led the crowd, perched high on his golden divan chair. Behind him walked hundreds of men in straight lines and behind them, three men—one dressed in a white robe. The men in the lines and columns each wore a gold medallion and carried a bronze censer.

The sun was a glaring red ball behind the Tabernacle as Korah and his followers took their places in it. The silver candlestick glinted reddishly in the rays of the rising sun. Moses and Aaron and all the spectators stood well ouside the area in front of the Holy Place and the Holy of Holies. Korah stood directly before the holy tent. Kevin and Moshe stood near Moses, no more than twenty feet from the candlestick, but the little tent was guarded as always by two armed sentries.

Korah raised one hand as the signal that he was about to begin. "Hear, O Lord of Israel. Hear the prayer of your people. Accept our service to you, the most High God. We bring you the finest offerings of the land: pure gold, incense from Egypt, and holy sacrifices. O Lord of Israel, be pleased with your servant Korah." Korah paused for a moment and then signaled to the men who stood behind the incense burners.

The three men walked stiffly through the columns, the man in the hooded white tunic walked a half pace in front of the others. Moshe watched the strange group. The men on either side of the man in white seemed to support or propel him forward, yet there was dignity in his step.

"Akohath!" cried Moshe mutely. *What are they doing to him? Not a sacrifice!*

No knives were drawn. No fire was lit under the altar. Moshe breathed a sigh of relief. One man removed himself to the far side, while the other stayed close to the hooded figure. Akohath stood upright, with head lifted. Moshe could tell that under the draping white tunic Akohath's arms were bound—perhaps he was gagged, too.

Korah put up his arms and prayed aloud, "Most High God of Israel, I consecrate before you this day, my son Akohath, to be the high priest under me." He turned to the men with censers. "Start burning the holy incense." Korah gave two sharp claps and a young boy with a silver spoon and a pouch of incense ran up." Korah took the spoon and dipped up the incense. Behind him and on both sides, all the other censer bearers repeated his gesture, taking the spoon from their attendants and filling it with the contents of the incense boxes.

Korah moved the spoon carefully and held it over the glowing coals of his censer. All the others did as he did.

The sky was free from clouds. Only a reddish haze hung over the Tabernacle from the rising sun.

That is why the first bolt of lightning came as such a surprise.

Moshe saw it from the corner of his eye.

A censer bearer to the left of Korah emptied his

spoon of incense onto the coals an instant before the others. As soon as the first grains hit the fiery embers a tearing flash of lightning ripped out of the cloudless sky and struck him down with an electric crack and the smell of burning cloth and flesh.

Already in motion and unable to stop, or not realizing what was happening, the other censer bearers turned over the little spoons.

One by one, as the grains of incense touched the coals, bolts of terrible blue-white fire fell from heaven to strike down the men that held the censers. Fire rained from the sky. The earth heaved and shook. The company of Korah's men fell to the flame. The ground opened and consumed the wives and children who had followed behind the incense burners.

The people who were faithful to Moses and Aaron stood transfixed. But after the first lightning bolt they covered their eyes.

"Quick, Kevin!" Moshe shouted. "This is our chance. Run for it."

Oblivious to the lightning falling about them, the boys sprinted toward the Holy Place.

What happened next takes longer in the telling than it did in the doing.

As Moshe and Kevin made the leap that they hoped would carry them through the frame under the menorah, the two awestruck guards reacted. The men clumsily, but quickly, brought the shafts of their javelins down hard on the heads and shoulders of the boys. Then the guards aimed their weapons properly and lunged to impale them.

With a wild shriek, Eber—poor mad Eber—rushed between the boys and the sentries and took the points intended for them.

In an instant of recognition, the tanner's wild eyes cleared and as Moshe and Kevin scrambled past the preoccupied guards, Eber called after them in his old voice.

"Good-bye, lads; good luck. Old Eber didn't forget!"

As they dived through the frame, Moshe and Kevin were caught in the rushing sound and light of the time vortex. Before the light grew so intense that it blotted out all forms, the boys looked back on the field of falling fire. Only one figure remained standing—the figure of Akohath still bound and standing straight as a ramrod. Behind him the baleful fire from heaven enveloped the 250 censer bearers. The boys watched the scene as if they were seeing a slow-motion instant replay. A streak of lightning shot toward Akohath, but instead of destroying him, it hit the cords that bound him and ricocheted. The bolt blazed across the open space and struck the silver menorah, shearing it off in a jagged point at the base, and sent it toppling down from the frame, onto the escaping time travelers. ...

"Quick, Kevin, I can't hold it!"

Kevin hurled himself forward to grab the toppling candlestick and broke its fall.

The roaring stopped; the light faded. Kevin and Moshe and the black-encrusted candlestick lay in a tangled heap of tarps and sawhorses on the floor of the Drummond storeroom.

"We're back," Kevin gasped.

"Thank God," said Moshe.

"Whatever," said Kevin. "I just know I'm glad to be back."

Moshe stared at his friend in disbelief.

"You mean that you have been through what we've been through and seen what we've seen and you can still pretend there isn't any God?!"

Kevin shrugged. "An earthquake and a thunderstorm. Big deal. They happen all the time."

"Oh, yeah?" retorted Moshe. "Then why did they kill just the bad guys? Natural disasters don't pick and choose. How come Akohath wasn't killed with the others? He was right smack in the middle of everything."

Kevin grinned. "I figure it must have had something to do with the conductivity of the incense they were using," he said grandly.

"Huh?" said Moshe.

"Sure," said Kevin. "The lightning was attracted to the incense."

Moshe hooted. "Conductivity, my hind foot," he laughed. "You still can't see the nose on your face, Kevin. Akohath didn't get struck by lightning because Akohath didn't break the Law! You can talk all you want about conductivity. Good intentions don't count with God. It's what you do that counts. And you know it. You said it yourself. If Akohath had sided with his father, he would have been a goner like all the others. Kevin, I think you're beginning to take God into your calculations!"

A rattle at the front of the store rescued Kevin from his embarrassment.

"Don't look now, Moshe," he said, "but these loincloths we're wearing don't seem to be able to take the twentieth century."

Moshe looked down. The loincloth he had put on in Korah's tent was crumbling to dust over his undershorts.

"Quick, grab a pair of coveralls," he hissed.

They grabbed at some work clothes hanging on the wall and got them on just as the door to the storeroom opened to admit Jack and Alice Leer.

"Hi, folks," said Kevin, "How'd you get in?"

Dr. Jack grinned. "Alan and Sue gave us a key so we could have the first look at the new batch of treasures from Kadesh-Barnea, but it looks like you two sleuths beat us to it. Anything interesting?"

The boys showed them the candlestick.

"Hmm," said Kevin's mother. "Silver oxide."

Dr. Jack laughed. "Not at all, Alice," he said with a wink at his son. "Can't you tell traces of fire from heaven when you see them?"

Dr. Alice laughed. "Moshe might fall for something like that," she said, "but not Kevin."

"I don't know about that," Moshe declared warmly. "Ask Kevin about the lightning bolt that ..." Moshe faltered. He saw Kevin put a finger up to his lips. It was their secret.

Dr. Alice laughed. "What lightning bolt? You two boys have vivid imaginations. That's good, but don't get carried away with that supernatural stuff. OK?"

"We won't," said Kevin agreeably.

"I should hope not," teased his mother. "I think Jack and I have brought you up better than that!"

Kevin put one arm around his mother and the other around his father. "I don't know, Mom," he smiled. "Like Dad always says, we should try to keep an open mind."